D1738735

GARDENS *of* GRIEF

GARDENS of GRIEF

a novel

BOSTON TERAN

Copyright 2010 by Brutus Productions, Inc.

All rights reserved under International and Pan American Copyright Conventions.

Library of Congress Control Number: 2010937933

Interior design by Neuwirth & Associates, Inc.

ISBN: 9781567030563

Published in the United States by High Top Publications LLC, Los Angeles, CA and simultaneously in Canada by High Top Publications LLC.

Dedicated to:

. . . the unnamed

. . . the unknown

. . . the lost

. . . the forgotten

. . . the imprisioned

. . . the tortured

. . . the murdered

. . . the slaughtered

. . .

Every man carries the history of the world in his soul—

This work is based on historical fact.

prologue

N JANUARY 1937, in the basement storage room of an old war department building, the files of the Creel Committee from 1917–1919 were discovered. These files were thought to be lost for twenty years, their whereabouts unknown even to the Library of Congress.

The Committee on Public Information was the most effective propaganda agency ever established in the United States. Among those lost files was a packet of notes, letters and reports by a special agent for the Bureau of Investigation, named John Lourdes.

PART I

The Journey

"BOSTON . . . SO RICH with history and meaning. Of all that is to be written about this great country . . . Boston will always be part of the first page."

The young lady at the podium speaking looked out upon an assembly of Americans that crowded Faneuil Hall. Her name was Alev Temple. It was not long after the beginning of the Great War. The air that night was heavy and many in the auditorium, and along the walls or squeezed in doorways, fanned themselves with fliers and contribution envelopes passed out upon their entering that celebrated meeting place.

She continued, "To stand at this podium, in this place known as the Cradle of Liberty, to be where Samuel Adams and the Sons of Liberty divined their historic opposition to British oppression, to realize the Boston Tea Party was conceived *here*, is an honor I wish, I so deeply wish, I had earned. But I have not."

The young woman took a moment and addressed her notes. The people were silent but for the occasional shuffling of paper or a lone cough, and for a few seconds she was afraid she would not find her voice.

"I am a young woman of twenty-two," she said, "who has achieved nothing to be worthy of this podium, or your presence. So, it would be right to ask, how did I come to be here?" She folded her hands and with dark, charged eyes looked out upon a nation of faces. "I am here because of my father, who was a doctor, and my mother, who was a nurse. Their . . . *murder* . . . was my passport to this podium. Their willingness to sacrifice their lives by living out the Christian code—I am my brother's keeper— is what allows me to be the voice of a people in desperate need of all our help.

"A people who are being driven from their homeland. Whose mothers and daughters, wives and sisters, are being violated, then butchered. Whose fathers and sons, husbands and brothers are being herded like beasts into the desert to be slaughtered.

"My father, not long before his death, said, "There is not a word in the English language to describe what is happening to those people. *Massacre* does not suffice . . . *annihilation* falls short. And if we, as a people, do not stand by "The Creed" our world is built upon, when it comes time a word is created to describe these unnameable atrocities, that word will also come to define the abject failure of our humanity."

two

*T*HERE IS NO greater simplicity than the stars. They cast no shadow, and they are forever. And for each and every man, they are the same.

John Lourdes stood on the deck of an old cargo steamer and looked out upon the secret darkness of the Black Sea. He was on that boat, in the spring of 1915, because he had agreed to become part of the larger enterprise known as war.

Far off into the night he could make out the first lights of Constantinople anchored along the horizon. With nothing beyond Texas and Mexico to his name, he had been cast upon the waters of the world.

It came to him quite suddenly, this feeling he had been emptied of the past, and any future tethered to it. That he had somehow slipped the bonds of personal history and birth and now somewhere beyond the silent shore of the new and unknown, he would come to define one John Lourdes.

⁓

JOHN LOURDES WATCHED dawn form across an Ottoman sky as they prepared to disembark. A great mosque with minarets like the lances of fabled titans shielded the light. There were boats everywhere with oddly hung sails and steamers making their way on toward the Caucasus. Anchored in the harbor were ships of the Turkish navy painted in that yellowish khaki, which he had over-heard in conversation concealed them against the coastline. From one of the minaret towers came the call to prayer. A figure in white robes appeared like a matchtip, the cadence of his song strange to John Lourdes' ears.

Like any traveler he disembarked and secured his luggage and hired a *hamal*—a porter. He had picked up a few words of Turkish during the trip. But even there, at the crossroads of the world, John Lourdes collected stares.

Maybe it was the Mallory hat, the western boots and canvas pants, the vest and shoulder holster. The hamal was handed two suitcases; one bore John Lourdes' clothes, the other articles of his trade. There were two scabbards, one housing a shotgun, the other a rifle.

The hamal asked in Turkish, in French, in German where he desired to be taken. John Lourdes answered in Spanish, "The Pera Palas Hotel . . . if you please." The *hamal* assumed he was a gentleman of importance and treated John Lourdes accordingly, *"Si, efendi, si."*

While on board ship he'd learned the hotel was considered a work of art, built by the French for travelers from Paris who had come to Constantinople on the Orient Express. The Pera Palas featured the first electric elevator in the city, and rumor had it a certain wealthy tycoon had been denied a suite of rooms because of "poor looks." It was there the U.S. State Department had instructed John Lourdes to take a room.

Speaking only Spanish, he made himself understood to the desk clerk. The paperwork he presented said he was a citizen of Mexico. He asked if there were any messages as he was expecting one. An envelope was handed to John Lourdes with his room key. As he was taken to the elevator his rifle scabbards drew the attention of passersby.

In his room he read the note carefully, then put it in the pocket notebook he carried with him. There would be nothing to do till nightfall but wait.

NOT LONG AFTER the Archduke had been assassinated and the beginning of the Great War, Justice Knox, the head of the Bureau of Investigation in El Paso, Texas, called one of his agents, John Lourdes, to a meeting.

It was not to be held at the Bureau offices, but at the home of the attorney, Wadsworth Burr. This was done to exact a measure of privacy. The meeting had been requested by a representative of the State Department.

The gentleman was a Harvard graduate and not much older than John Lourdes. "No matter what the outcome of this meeting," he said in advance, "it is to be understood everything discussed is a matter of national security. And, as such, to be held in the strictest confidence."

The representative from Washington had an even temperament and spoke with austere urgency about a plague of overseas concerns facing the government. State was recruiting men from Customs, the Bureau of Investigation, the military, to be stationed throughout Europe and the Ottoman Empire to work clandestinely as information gatherers and couriers. They were to be an advance guard, a reconnaissance force, so to speak. A lifeline of intelligence to help the government understand and evaluate events on the ground and so better confront evolving crises. It was also to be a means for advising the Entente in the conflict.

It was to be understood the agent would almost certainly be faced with questionable situations, unexpected adversaries, the unknown intentions of associates, confrontations beyond the pure dangers of the war itself.

These would demand the agent have considerable acuity and, by necessity, be capable of making swift and determinative decisions. The representative then added, precautions would be put in place to protect the agent. At least, as was humanly possible.

"Your record, Mr. Lourdes, caught our eye. Your time in Mexico with that assassin." The man from the State Department paused a moment. "But it was your background that we felt would make you particularly useful to us."

"My background?"

"The fact, Mr. Lourdes, that you're not white."

FROM HIS HOTEL window John Lourdes could look down upon the historic harbor known as the Halic, though Westerners called it the Golden Horn. He walked the quay, teeming it was with people. His intention was to kill the hours before the appointed meeting where he was to receive his orders. In truth, the walk was to clear his mind.

Merchant stalls lined the vast estuary. An infinite passageway of day to day treasures, a living dream to the nearness of the world, and the ultimate temptation to man's incurable limitations. Yet, there was one aspect to this place of manifest antiquity that could not escape the traveler. It was not white.

The Greek had harbored there, the Roman, the Byzantine, and the Ottoman. The Crusader had left his mark, as had the Jew and the Muslim. The Halic had been witness to tumult and wars and was the subject of endless works of art. "And if you recall your mythology," Wadsworth Burr had told John Lourdes upon his departure, "Jason's hunt for the Golden Fleece."

As he had climbed the gangway John Lourdes yelled back, "I'll keep an eye out for it!" But then, he took a moment and looked toward Burr. They had years and John Lourdes' father between them. "I know what you're telling me, Wadsworth. And thanks."

Before the war, intelligence had come mostly from missionaries, consuls, and involved nationals. Their information was passed on through letters and encrypted messages. Since the war encryptions were being deciphered and the mails read by the authorities. That's why State brought in John Lourdes and others, who like him, didn't measure out their lives half a glass at a time.

Far down the quay there was a sudden commotion. German officers leading a squad of Turkish gendarmes from stall to stall. John Lourdes watched them leave a trail of havoc in their wake.

A panic began to spread among the crowd. There were shouts, an oddly pitched whistle. The gendarmes had drawn their weapons. People scattered across the quay as a man in a plain kaftan burst through the crowd. He was sprinting in John Lourdes' direction, using his forearms and elbows to drive apart bodies and make his escape.

A German officer was pointing at him. There followed a battery of shots. The air crackled with pistol fire. The whole of the quay was swept up in the moment. The man's face was strained with the running and the fear. It looked as if he might elude the gendarmes when there was a flashpoint of blackened dust on the front of his kaftan from where the bullet had exited.

His body was driven forward. A sandal flew loose. He stumbled to his knees. Blood from the wound drained onto the stones beneath his slumping shadow. From somewhere a woman cried out, her voice a pitched fury. Space formed around the man, people stood and watched in disbelief the dying. The gendarmes closed in with guns drawn.

The man looked up. John Lourdes was a body length away.

The eyes in the darkened face saw and understood the calamity that had befallen it. One arm rose and stretched out. Was it the useless gesture of a man already dead, or something else—?

A quick succession of gunshots drove him to the stones. A queer and unsettling quiet spread along the quay. The Turkish police tried to move the bystanders on. This should have been the end of it, but it was not.

The woman who had been screaming was held at bay by a German officer, but it was another woman that caught John Lourdes' attention. In cloak and veil she slipped through the crowd. Small, silent, near invisible. Her arms were tight against her body where she protected a child in swaddling cloth.

She took lean, quick steps, approaching a different German officer near the body. He was caught off guard by this woman clutching a child and put up an indifferent hand for her to stop. But she did not.

In the path of a few seconds, the world can make itself known. What John Lourdes saw, the German by the body saw, and he understood what was about to befall him, but too late. In the swaddling cloth was not a child, but the wooden stick and thin sheet metal of a grenade.

At the moment of the blast the woman and the German were so close as to be one agonizing embrace. The two nearest gendarmes were pierced through with wood and metal shards. Their wounds bright pools and slash marks on the gray stone where they lay. Someone shouted a word John Lourdes did not understand: *Fedayeen!*

three

*J*OHN LOURDES SAT in the hotel lobby that night waiting for his contact. He wrote in his pocket notebook, as was his method, the events of the day.

A word he had not understood—*fedayeen*—pronouncing it as best he could, he asked a gentleman behind the front desk to please write it out for him, and explain its meaning. The clerk, an older and rather refined looking fellow, did as he was asked, then staring at John Lourdes indignantly answered, "It means . . . blasphemous murderers."

Though he neither grasped or fully appreciated the meaning of what he had witnessed on the quay, it was the stark political barbarity that said to John Lourdes some new level of infamy was being ushered into the world. And that if you were not prepared for it, you would be put under by it.

And yet, in the hotel lobby one would hardly be aware the incident on the quay had happened at all. Ladies and their gentlemen, all elegantly dressed, waited to dine or for carriages to take them to the theater. The ladies stood together and gossiped, the men regaled about business or themselves. It was as if their private world, was the world, thought John Lourdes.

"Efendi?"

John Lourdes looked up from his notebook.

A tallish man in a long coat, who seemed to be of Arab and Chinese blood said, "The manager," he pointed to the front desk, "said you are Mr. Lourdes. Is that right?"

He nodded, and stood.

"I'm here to take you to Mr. Baptiste—"

"Mr. Baptiste was supposed to—"

"There is trouble in the streets tonight. It is not safe."

As they crossed the lobby, a number of men who had been at the bar, including one with a tripod and camera, rushed past. The hotel was a notorious crossroads for news and was never short of international reporters and magazine writers.

A crowd was gathering on the hotel steps as John Lourdes exited the lobby. Coming through the parked *arabas* and automobiles was a young woman with dark hair and darker charged eyes. She was carrying a torch in one hand and a rolled up cloth in the other. She led a small train of children in peasant clothes. Each carried a lit candle in one hand, while cupping the flame with the other to protect it against the breeze off the Black Sea. A few women followed behind them and one John Lourdes recognized from her tragic fit of tears on the quay.

The young woman with the torch took up a place at the entry facing the street and had the children squeeze in close so the light from the lobby fell around them. Reporters had begun throwing their questions at her but, despite her youth, she remained composed and silent, till the tripod was set up and the camera ready.

"A man was murdered today," she said. "He was shot down within sight of this hotel." John Lourdes could pick up the slightest trace of a British accent. "He was murdered for two reasons. One, he was a political writer. And two, he was an Armenian. Those were his crimes against the Empire."

The man escorting John Lourdes tugged at his coat sleeve, "Efendi, we must hurry."

"These are his children," said the young woman. "And that one is his sister. They, too, are fated to be killed."

John Lourdes followed his escort through the crowd and away from the hotel and looked back only when there came a collective gasp from the crowd.

The bundled-up cloth the young woman had been carrying was, in fact, the dead man's kaftan. It hung now from her free hand like a shroud, grim and bloody in torchlight.

JOHN LOURDES WAS being led up into the Beyoglu by his nameless escort who walked quickly, watching always, anxious, intent, for there were gendarmes everywhere that night and they had retribution on their mind.

It was the European quarter they were entering, with its embassies and stone mansions and Arabic palaces from before the written word. Along the Grand Rue de Pera the authorities patroled the streets in squads of two and three with lanterns, stopping tourists and searching arabas. The man motioned to John Lourdes to indicate they would avoid the well-lit causeways.

"Is it because of what happened on the quay?" whispered John Lourdes.

"The Turk is hunting the Armenian. Writers . . . teachers . . . churchman . . . The Turk means to kill them all. Some are being hidden in this quarter."

John Lourdes followed this shadow figure up through passageways of cobber stone and caryatids, scurrying from any lights that would suddenly flare across the gray walls in the hunt for alcoves and alleyways where the Armenian might hide.

"In these times," whispered the man, "it is better to be a Jew."

THEY TURNED INTO a street no wider than a handcart. Faceless two-story rowhouses up stepped cobblestone. Bare, but for a few rosettes of window light. A child's voice here, a man's there. And the smells, each its own intense and unknown island to John Lourdes' senses.

They came to a heavy wooden door and the man with John Lourdes knocked. After a time the eyelatch opened, a momentary set of eyes appeared, silhouetted by a gas lamp on the wall. The eyelatch closed. The door eased in on its bracings.

A woman, backlit in the entry. Tall, Arabic. A red kaftan fell loose to her bare feet. The man spoke to her and all John Lourdes understood was: "Mr. Baptiste . . ."

When the women stepped back into the entry, John Lourdes saw her face was marked with blue ink on her chin and cheeks and brow. The man did not enter with John Lourdes.

"This is as far as I go," he said. "May your god watch over you."

His new guide led him down a corridor of beaded doorways where women served men their pipes and sat with them naked in the opaque luxury of pillows piled deep as clouds. Women from Africa, Arab women, Caucasian women, women of unidentifiable origin, all with the same blue markings.

He followed the woman up a stairway to where the walls were lined with tapestries. The story of Ali Baba woven from centuries of silk. With scimitars and white steeds and a slave girl dancing with a dagger, all gleaming in gaslight. A horde of thieves on horseback trampling under the world ran the length of one corridor to a final beaded doorway where the flickery light of a projector cast its smoky mark upon the eyes.

She stood by a stairway to the roof and pointed. That was where John Lourdes was to go.

Mr. Baptiste was sitting on the roof wall. He rose as John Lourdes approached. "From the ruins of the old palace, I saw you coming," he said.

Mr. Baptiste wore a European suit and tie, there was even the perfunctory handkerchief in the upper coat pocket. He had a long wide face that appeared flat and lineless, and the eyes too were set wide. It looked to John Lourdes to be a face easily frightened.

They shook hands.

"I hope I didn't insult by bringing you to this place. It was a matter of safety. My own, primarily. I'm Armenian, you see."

"Opium smells the same everywhere."

"Have you ever been to this part of the world before?"

"No."

"What do you think? So far?"

John Lourdes paused, then smiled. "It ain't Texas," he said.

Mr. Baptiste grinned. "I felt the same when I first went to England. College. It was so gray. So formal. And the way people looked and spoke at me. I wrote my father. Begged he let me come home. You could imagine what a father would say to that."

"I could imagine what mine would say . . . As long as you're there, Mr. Lourdes, find a way to rob the Queen."

John Lourdes sat. He looked out over a kingdom of rooftops and minarets that fell away to the black of the Black Sea.

"It's quite beautiful, until you realize what it means."

John Lourdes did not understand.

"The lights." He pointed.

Mr. Baptiste hadn't meant the long rivery lines of the street lamps, but those small cadres of the gendarmerie searching the Beyoglu.

"The murder on the quay."

"You heard?"

"I was there."

Mr. Baptiste sat close to John Lourdes.

"Is that what all this is for?" said John Lourdes.

"No. Today was just an excuse."

"How do you mean?"

"You're Mexican I was told, but of the United States."

"That's right. Mexican and American."

"Is it as hard to be a Mexican in the United States as it is to be African?"

"We were never put in chains. So, no."

"But you're not considered white?" Mr. Baptiste took an envelope from his coat pocket. "An Armenian is the African of this country. Between us and the Turk there are differences. Social, political, historical, religious. The Turk is fundamentally Muslim, the Armenian Christian. That is why the Turk has so much resentment of the missionary. To him they are the servant of Europe and America and allies of the Armenian. And the Turk means to have the Armenian dead."

Mr. Baptiste ran the edge of the envelope between his fingers. "These are your . . . orders. Before I hand them over to you . . . does the name Calouste Gulbenkian mean anything to you?"

"I'm afraid it doesn't."

"He is an architect of business and a financial broker. Born Armenian, he is also a British citizen. And a patriot. He put the merger together that became Royal Dutch-Shell . . . That merger helped fuel the British Navy. He's been the voice and soul of the Baku. Do you know the Baku?"

"The oil fields on the Caspian Sea."

"Your record, I am told, indicates you spent time in the Mexican oil fields for the BOI."

"Tampico."

"The Baku dwarfs Tampico. Half the oil that comes out of the ground is from the Baku. The Baku will fuel the future. And the German, through the Turk can not—"

John Lourdes rose abruptly. "Over there!"

He had been looking out across the rooftops while Mr. Baptiste spoke. Threads of illumination were closing in on the near end of the block.

four

"WE MUST LEAVE HERE."

Mr. Baptiste did not start toward the stairwell, but rather set off across the roof at a run, keeping low. He scuttled up onto the ledge that connected buildings then dropped down to the next roof. He moved silently with John Lourdes following, from building to building. Suddenly at their end of the street, cutting through the blind dark, was another squad of gendarmes. The narrow cobble walkway flaring up before their lights. Realizing they might have to make a stand right there, John Lourdes reached for his automatic in its shoulder holster. Mr. Baptiste put a hand out to refrain him.

"No," he said. "Come."

Mr. Baptiste, near crawling now, made his way to a roof hatch. He struggled to lift the heavy wooden cover. It opened onto a black space that descended into the building.

"A ladder," said Mr. Baptiste. "I first, you follow. Be careful. The wood is old."

The ladder creaked gravely under John Lourdes' boots. He had to feel his way with a foot to know when he reached the floor. It was dark, the air rank with must. The faint echo of their movements told him the building was empty. Mr. Baptiste took him by the arm and guided him to a landing and down a flight of faulty stairs.

They proceeded along a passage that ended at thin bands of light. It was a door where the moon slipped through its loose and battered slat. Enough moon for each man to make out the barest details of the other.

Mr. Baptiste took a pocket revolver from his coat. "Beyond this door . . . I'm sorry. I will do my best. I promise."

The gendarmes were close, there was fire in their voices.

Mr. Baptiste held out the envelope. "By taking this . . . You must understand. You are being entrusted with our faith."

John Lourdes saw fragments of the man's face through the shadows. He had been wrong about Mr. Baptiste. His was not a face easily frightened, quite the contrary. It was a face calmly prepared for all eventualities.

John Lourdes accepted the letter. "You will not find me wanting . . . efendi."

Mr. Baptiste nodded. "There is an alley straight across the walkway. It is where we . . . you . . . will go. If you end up alone—"

Mr. Baptiste took hold of the door handle. He hesitated, "My wife," he said, "as I left tonight . . . she said she would wait up for me."

He pulled the door open and both men sprinted across the walkway. A shot registered shortly thereafter and its echo rolled up that long and lightless alley where they fled. John Lourdes could feel the walls on both sides of him, and when he reached the far boulevard Mr. Baptiste was nowhere to be found. Out of breath, he looked back. There was an assault of gunfire from far down that dark passway between dwellings.

At the harbor that morning John Lourdes had observed the gendarmes carried not only short sabers for crowd control but Mauser sidearms. They were big and clunky pieces of craftsmanship, but they delivered on firepower. He couldn't make out shadows or any sign of barrel flashes. He just heard a staccato run of shots, and they weren't courtesy of a pocket revolver.

~

IN THE ENVELOPE was a letter. Following its instructions, the next day John Lourdes boarded, *Le Minotaur*, a coal paddlewheeler heading for the port city of Trebizond on the far eastern shore of the Black Sea. He was to be met by a scout, a guide of sorts, to take him on into the *vilayets*—the frontier provinces. The reason for his journey was to be held in the strictest of confidence.

The mission was to reach a priest by the name of Malek. The Turkish War Department under Enver Pasha had put a bounty on his head. Once captured, he was to become the property of the Teskilat-I-Mahsusa, the Special Organization, for Malek was much more than a holy man. John Lourdes was to serve as envoy, helping to organize and insure the priest's safe passage to the city of Van.

Van was a centerpiece of the resistance. Many of the Freedom Party and the National Liberation Movement were there. Fighting was intense in and around Van. The Armenians controled part of the city, but were trapped there, and under daily siege by the Turkish Army and militia and their German advisors.

The State Department also had men there who wanted to meet with Malek and others of the resistance to determine and coordinate a course of action to support the Entente and defeat the Central Powers.

The letter, written by Mr. Baptiste and containing these instructions, also had a terse postscript: Luke 10, 25–37.

John Lourdes was on shaky ground when it came to his Bible passages, so he copied chapter and verse in his pocket notebook for a later time. He then took the letter, and as instructed, tore it up. He threw the remains into the foamy wake left by the side-wheeler's paddle.

He took to watching the sea, and it wasn't long before a small gray craft became visible, pressing through the ropy waters and running parallel to the steamer about a half mile off the port side. He cupped a hand over his eyes to better see what she was.

"It's German . . . A patrol boat."

He turned in the direction of the voice. She was about a dozen paces up the deck railing. It was the woman from the night before on the hotel steps, the one with the torch and bloody kaftan.

"How can you tell?" said John Lourdes.

She approached him, still looking out to sea. "I saw one once just off the coast near Sinope attack a trawler, then set it and everyone on board on fire."

She was younger looking than what he thought the night before. One might even suggest more innocent. Her skin was quite swarthy, yet her nose was aquiline. She now gave him her full attention.

"Your speech," she said. "American?"

"Texas. Though I'm a citizen of Mexico."

"Texas is a very large state, is it not?"

"Larger than that."

She smiled appreciatively.

"I haven't seen very much of America. I was in Boston recently, on a fundraising tour for the Relief Agency."

"You have a touch of a British accent," he said.

"My father was British, my mother Turkish. I was born in Baku."

From the deck above came shouting. German officers traveling to Trebizond called and waved to their own on the patrol boat.

"They think they've already won the war," said the young woman.

One of the German officers on board shot up a flare. The sky above hissed and streamered red. Moments later the patrol boat answered and the sky there streaked with phosphor.

"I saw you last night," said John Lourdes, "at the hotel."

"Were you one of those offended by my display, or—?"

"I was on the quay when the murder took place."

"You saw—"

"Yes. As close as we were when you first spoke to me."

Friends of the young woman now called to her from up near the prow. She signaled with a wave she would be with them momentarily.

"I work for the International Relief Agency." She put out a hand. "My name is Alev Temple." She spelled Alev for him. "It is a Turkish name."

He shook her hand. "John Lourdes."

"What is taking you to Trebizond, John Lourdes?"

Offhandedly, he remarked, "A religious matter."

She accepted that. But as she started off to her friends said, "I assume that explains the weapons you were carrying in those scabbards, when you boarded."

A BITTER ARGUMENT arose that evening in the lounge, pitting the young relief worker against the German officer in charge. It was he who had sent up the flare that morning to his brothers in arms in the patrol boat. Since John Lourdes had been aft smoking, he did not know how or when the argument began.

The lounge was full that evening, and other passengers stood in the entry or watched from the deck through the glass windows as Miss Temple and Rittmeister Bodo Franke vehemently had at each other.

"Don't tell me I didn't understand what you were saying. I speak Turkish."

"And speak you do," said Rittmeister Franke.

Miss Temple pointed to a table where two of his brother officers sat, along with three members of the Turkish military who were with the Special Organization.

"These men and yourself were discussing the extermination—"

"Deportation of the Armenian contingent within Turkish borders."

"Why are the Germans here? To oversee—"

"To protect the sovereignty of the Turkish government from internal agitators and outside aggressors. Such as the Russian, the British, the—"

Miss Temple raised her voice. "My father and mother were murdered by men such as these in the Special Organization. They once took an English dictionary from my father and because it had words in it such as 'liberty' and 'freedom,' they burned it. And every paper, every document, every letter, newspaper article, his Bible, maps, anything with the word 'Armenia' on it . . . they burned." She paused, "Then one night they came and burned my father and mother."

28

"How many languages do you speak, Miss Temple?"

"Excuse me?"

"How many languages?"

"Two. Turkish and English."

Rittmeister Franke stood with his hands folded behind his back. When he spoke, his speech did not carry the usual aggressive, self-aggrandizing manner of the cavalry commander. His tone was more that of an attorney honorably prosecuting his case.

"You speak two languages. Well, let me tell you. Any fool can speak one language . . . All you have to do is be born. Two languages . . . Everyone has two parents, so there is ample opportunity. Three languages are where you start to prove how educated, intelligent, and knowledgeable you are. Miss Temple, you are a language short."

"In Van," said Miss Temple. "When Armenian Christians are brought before the governor, he likes to put them in small cage like cells and turn hungry, wild cats upon them. Cats meant to attack, bite, claw at the victim."

"Propaganda begat by lies," said Rittmeister Franke.

"Lies begat to hide the facts," answered Miss Temple.

"The relief workers have proven themselves to be nothing more than a propaganda arm of the British government."

"The missions are filled with orphans. That is not propaganda."

"Who finances the relief worker? British wealth, the British industrialist. Their aim. The oil fields of Baku and Basra. They want to control the fuel to feed their navy because they are a dying power without it."

"What is the Berlin to Baghdad Railway? What is the Batum to Baku pipeline? It is the means by which the German army can fuel its run to empire."

"The Turkish government and the German government are allies, and as such entered into an open arrangement."

"You want the Armenian gone because he is a Christian, because he wants a free and open—"

"Why are there more British soldiers here than in Europe? Why? The oil. The Royal Dutch-Shell merger, who owns those companies? What is the power behind those companies? The British government—"

A man cried out, "Dear God!"

He was standing near the prow. "There's a body," he shouted, to those turning toward him.

The lounge emptied. The captain's mate scuttled down the forecastle steps.

"It was there!" he said, pointing to the waterline.

The passengers pressed up against the railing to see. Alev Temple found herself alongside John Lourdes. There was nothing but the sound of the engines and the slopping tread of water. Then, in the long course of quiet seconds rising out of the white lappings behind the paddlewheel, a corpse all glimmery wet and naked. People along the railing yelled out, they called to the mate. The swollen torso hit against the hull with a thud then was taken by the aftertow off into the night.

Disquiet settled in along the deck. The mate called up to the forecastle that there was another body sighted. It was two ship lengths or so away from the vessel on the port side.

The passengers searched the low black waves. One pointed to where a casket of naked flesh rose and fell with the current. It was a stark imprisoning vision, and someone questioned could it be a wreck was out there in the night.

John Lourdes had Alev Temple ask the mate if the ship carried flares to search the dark, and the mate answered that the second had neglected to provide for a new supply. John Lourdes then turned to Rittmeister Franke. "Captain," he said, "could you see your way to—"

"I'll expend no flares on the dead."

Nothing more was debated. John Lourdes turned and walked away. In his tiny cabin, he ticked up the gas lamp. He took the suitcase containing the articles of his trade and lay it on the bed.

When John Lourdes returned, one of the Turkish officers noticed he was carrying a flare gun and a handful of flares. The officer called this to the attention of Rittmeister Franke. "Sir," Rittmeister Franke said, "you are being advised not to use that flare."

"Miss Temple," said John Lourdes, "please ask the first mate if any of these gentlemen have authority here."

She did as requested. The mate called up to the captain who was leaning into the forecastle railing.

She relayed the answer back to John Lourdes, "They have no authority."

He loaded up the flare.

The same Turkish officer spoke out again. Rittmeister Franke said nothing. John Lourdes saw the Turkish officer's hand came to rest on the wooden holster that housed his Mauser.

"Captain Franke," said John Lourdes, "if you would be so kind as to notify the officer I am a citizen of Mexico. Then ask him, if he has ever seen anyone accidentally shot at close range with a flare gun."

Rittmeister Franke and the officer exchanged words for several strained minutes. The matter was resolved without incident.

John Lourdes stepped to the railing. He had Miss Temple move aside, then he fired off a flare where the last body had been seen.

White phosphor lit the sky and there, ferried on the black deeps, were the dead.

Not one or two, but a ghostway covering waves. Like white statuary they floated weightless while the sea washed over them.

"Why," someone whispered, "are they all naked?"

five

THE PORT OF Trebizond was an emporia from
before Xenophon and the Greek wars with Persia. It has been
called the "City of Tales" and from its citadel walls Marco Polo
looked out upon the legendary Silk Road, where caravans carried
their treasures across the deserts of antiquity. But on the morning
Le Minotaur made dock, Trebizond was an armed encampment of
the Turkish military.

Transports lined the harbor, each throwing a shadow across the
deck of the next. Howitzers on plank rafts were hoisted by high
derricks from ship holes. Along the quay infantry brigades organized on streets teeming with horse-drawn carts and wagons and
dull gray trucks. The ground there spotted with horse droppings
and human filth. Even the sea air could not clean away the stench
that comes with men at war.

Amidst the chaotic traffic John Lourdes collected up his belongings on the dock by *Le Minotaur.*

Miss Temple called to him, "John Lourdes!"

She was coming down the gangway and no longer dressed as a young lady. She wore heavy cotton breeches and laced-up boots. A weathered knapsack was slung over one shoulder, and her black hair lay hidden beneath a plain scarf.

"Miss Temple."

"There's something I'd like to ask." Her tone grew more serious. "A favor."

Before she could explain, Rittmeister Franke walked over and joined them. "Miss Temple. I want to thank you for the spirited debate."

"If only I could have done more," she said, rather caustically.

"I stopped to give you news." He offered Alev Temple a newspaper. "The British fleet has been defeated in the Dardanelles. A dozen ships lay destroyed in the straights. The assault has failed." He turned to John Lourdes. "As a citizen of Mexico, maybe one day, with my country's help, your rightful homeland will belong to you."

She took from him the Turkish newspaper. It was replete with eyewitness accounts of the fighting. The headline:

BRITISH SHIPS LEFT BURNING IN THE SEA.

One report described the battle as a defining moment in Turkish history.

The captain joined a group of officers on horseback. A saddled mount awaited. He rose in the stirrups expertly. "Miss Temple," he said, "I heard you are on your way to Van. I, too. Expect fighting there."

The Turkish officers from the night before rode up and joined the Germans, and Alev Temple watched them with grave concern as they all rode off.

"The favor," said John Lourdes.

She turned to him.

"Whatever brought you to this country . . . whatever the true reason, you are often writing in a notebook. I wish you to keep a record of what you see. Take last night. Make a living record you can give to a consul, a missionary, or even a relief worker like myself. It is in this way we are trying to get the truth out. The truth of what is going on here. Last night for instance."

"What about last night?"

"I believe you have an idea. I think you sensed what horror had occurred. Which is why you went and brought back the flare."

"But I still don't know what it was."

"I say, last night is what the government defines as . . . deportation."

The relief fund missionaries she was traveling with called to her from the gangway as they descended. She put out a hand to say good-bye.

"If kismet means for us to meet again, I have a slight request."

He regarded her closely, "Please."

"You will call me Alev, so I may call you John."

They shook hands.

She said something to him in Turkish and started away. It sounded deeply felt, even touching. He wanted to ask what it meant, but did not. It was the not knowing that most intrigued him.

⌒

THE GUIDE WHO was supposed to meet John Lourdes at the dock—did not. He set his larger suitcase upright and used it as a seat and waited. He felt the sweat of worry accumulate on the back of his neck. He drank a street peddler's coffee that went down like warm tar and watched endless lines of badly outfitted infantry march by.

Thoughts about his father came to him. He tried to trace the thoughts back to the headwaters of why. Why at that moment?

Then the ghost of Rawbone filing his teeth for a picture perfect grin flashed across his consciousness and it all became clear. I am near thirty years old and halfway around the world in the middle of a war, thought John Lourdes. At about the same age, that outlaw *malabarista* father of mine had been in Manila, in another war, at another time, halfway around the world.

"Efendi . . . ?"

Caught off guard, John Lourdes came about. A man stood before him in raggedy clothes and scarred fez. If there ever was a living piece of human gristle, this fellow was it.

"Mr. Baptiste sent me, if you are the John Lourdes."

"I am."

John Lourdes stood. He was near a head taller. The little man was paper thin, with bones like small knots of bark just beneath the flesh.

"I watched. To know it's safe. I have horses." He pointed up the street.

He was a fidgety bastard, and constantly running a finger across his lower lip. He grabbed up the rifle scabbards and one of the suitcases and asked John Lourdes to follow.

"What do they call you?" said John Lourdes.

The fellow rattled off a train load of names John Lourdes could not even repeat, let alone remember. "Best to call me Hain. That is the name I am known by. It was given to me in prison. By friends." He smiled. "It means . . . rat."

Half to himself, John Lourdes uttered, "Why doesn't that surprise me?"

"Excuse, efendi?"

"Nothing. You speak English pretty well."

"Missionary school. You know missionaries. Teach you—beat you. Beat you—teach you." He spit in contempt. "My name also means renegade . . . Judas . . . scoundrel."

"What to bet you've earned that name."

"What good is one you haven't?"

Three horses were posted outside a waterfront tavern and watched over by an old wretch who sat on the ground beside them. In one socket the pupil floated there like a blue film.

Two of the mounts looked to have done hard time. "My horse . . . pack horse," said Hain. But the third mount, "An Arab," said Hain.

The Arab was a pure creation. Courage and endurance not its only trademarks. John Lourdes looked from withers to croup.

"The *jibbah*," said Hain, running his fingers along the shield between the eyes. "And the *mitbah*," he said as he caressed the neck. "Very fine. Mr. Baptiste gave me a good deal of money to see you had the right horse."

John Lourdes recalled reading the Arab had been brought to Europe when the Moor invaded the Iberian Peninsula. He gave Hain a hard look. "I'll bet you pocketed the money and stole the horse."

HAIN HAD BEEN paid to lead John Lourdes to a village named Sophia, which lay about ninety kilometers southeast of the harbor. He was also to serve as interpreter. He asked many questions about the journey, which John Lourdes did not answer. The guide's curiosity, though, was unwavering.

The road cut its way through terrain that reminded John Lourdes of the western Rockies. On their ascent he could make out a train of foot soldiers moving toward crescent mountains in the east. Just beyond was Kars, where the Russian bear awaited. Another army of Turkish troops assembled at the base of Boztepe Hill. Its advance guard already had begun the drive south to Baghdad and the oil fields of Basra to check the British advance.

As they rode through the blue shadow of hills the guide waved a hand across the wild and barren country. "The tribesmen here fought the Roman. They poisoned them with a drink brewed from honey. It made the Roman see monsters and demons."

John Lourdes thought a moment about this, "They have a drink like that where I come from."

"Yes, efendi . . . How is it called?"

"Tequila."

He nodded at this new knowledge. From his coat pocket he took a battered *chibouk*. In a snakeskin pouch he kept a harsh, black tobacco. This he stuffed down into the pipebowl with fingers caked in dirt.

Stooping in the saddle, he smoked. They rode in silence until John Lourdes asked, "What is your background . . . Your nationality?"

"I am a Turk, when I need to be . . . A Muslim when I have to be, which is often . . . I am an Armenian when I need to be . . . I am even a stinking Kurd when necessary . . . But I am never a Jew." He pointed the tip of the *chibouk* down to his crotch. "The belt around the head of the snake, if that is not missing, one cannot well lie about being a Jew."

He spit dryly and wiped his mouth with the back of his hand.

He was about to question John Lourdes again on the purpose of the journey when they came upon a legion of peasants adrift on a road that was consumed with their dust.

Women and children all, and not an adult male among them. Being driven by Turkish guards and the scrabble of hooves. Moving off into the high grass John Lourdes and the guide eased their mounts past peasants carrying their belongings in meager bindles or strapped to their backs. They were a grave and haggard lot covered with flies.

"The deportations," whispered Hain.

The guards kept the walkers in hard order with uncompromising cruelty, but even under that, hunger ruled. A boy broke loose and rushed John Lourdes. He grabbed at his pant leg, pleading.

A moment later it was all madness. Other children, women, some too withered to bear up, charged toward the two men. The guide fared no better than John Lourdes. Their horses shied then panicked, the pack mount stumbled. The guards breeched the mob with a fury, beating their ranks back with rifles, trampling them.

six

*T*HEY CAMPED THAT night high up off the road on a cleft amidst great stones that had once been part of a Mithraic temple. Hain cooked strips of goat meat on sticks while John Lourdes sat with his back against a rock and wrote in his notebook.

"Today, on the road, I heard people saying the same words over and over."

"Ahh, yes," said Hain. "Hungry, hungry . . . please. The Armenian learns fast how to beg."

"Where were the men? Do you know?"

"Deported. But you cannot give the Armenian too much sympathy, efendi."

John Lourdes looked up from his notebook.

"If the world were different," said his companion, "they would be the Turk. And besides, they are a filthy people." Squatting there he turned the meat in the flame and wiped at the sweat on his face with a ragged sleeve. "You must not shake an Armenian's hand. And do you know why?"

"I do not."

"Because it is the hand he wipes his ass with. The truth. And they do not wash the hand afterwards. Also the truth." His tone grew more resolute, more sharp. "They cannot be trusted. Especially their hooked-nose women to the marriage vows. I know this from personal experience."

He held out a stick with meat for John Lourdes, who looked at it, then asked, "Which hand do you wipe your ass with?"

The guide's face took on a wily grin, and the firelight shined on the black holes in his mouth where once were teeth. "Know too, efendi, the Armenian does not dream. This was taken from him by his god for sins committed against the Turk."

John Lourdes took the meat and some raisins in a bowl and ate. "Hain, what does the word *fedayeen* mean?"

The little man thought the question curious and regarded John Lourdes just so. "Soldier . . . but not soldier. Fighter."

"And what do you know of a man named Malek?"

The guide had been about to eat, but this query caused him true concern. "Malek. The angel." He stared into the flames, his face grew strangely ambiguous. "The soldier priest." He shook his head. "They say he dragged a Turkish officer into his church and before his people he hacked off the man's head. He then said mass."

Both men went back to eating without a word more. The fire gradually drew itself upon the fallen rocks in shadow. Finally Hain could not contain his need and raised a voice, "Efendi . . . is he the journey?"

THAT NIGHT A fog came to the hills. Pale as bone it slipped along the earth. From across the smoky embers the guide watched John Lourdes' bedroll and in that slow, damp covering he slithered off to where the mounts were staked. He eased away a suitcase and on that silent hillside began to search. He kept staring at the bedroll and so was startled when a light fell about the gray air around him.

Light and man had magicked out of nowhere.

He looked to the bedroll. It lay still in a stream of gray mist. He turned to face John Lourdes. "I am ashamed, efendi. It was only my need to know . . . Is the soldier priest the journey?"

John Lourdes switched off the light. "What should shame you," he said, "is being so easily caught."

⌒

THE TOWN OF Sophia was roughly nine kilometers west of Erzurum on a silent cart path up through a rugged gash in the hills. The fog still rode about the horses' shoulders giving way in a ghostly manner as they proceeded.

"You did not answer last night? About the soldier priest."

"But I did answer," said John Lourdes.

"Your silence, then."

John Lourdes said no more.

"Efendi, you will die far from home."

He thought for a time on this and considered telling Hain about a certain priest, who in his old age, had come to Texas from Sinaloa. He had crossed the same Mexican desert as had John Lourdes' mother to begin a new life. The priest often told the people of his parish in El Paso, one of whom was a boy named John Lourdes, "Everywhere I go, I bring my home with me." In the end, he did not tell this to the guide, for he felt it would not matter.

43

They came upon the town quite suddenly. A few sloping blocks of low rooftops rising above the mist. They rode a dirt street lined with empty windows and open doorways. The buildings were mud-brick and timber and to John Lourdes' way of thinking, this is what would be called in Texas a hard scrabble existence. At the end of the street was a little square with a town well and a trough. Here they dismounted and let the horses drink.

Facing the square was a church. And as in the west of John Lourdes, the poorer the town, the richer the church. It was not mud-brick but rather blocks of stone irregularly cut with doors and windows framed in ashlar.

"Efendi," said the guide. He was standing at the church entrance and pointing to a *khatchkar* embedded into the wall. John Lourdes walked up beside him.

"This is an Armenian town. It says here . . . 1740."

John Lourdes looked. Chiseled into the rock was a cross with rays emanating from it. There was writing and the date.

"The people we saw on the road," said John Lourdes. "They could have been taken from here."

"We should leave, efendi."

"Walk the town on that side. Every house."

The guide did as he was told, but reluctantly. John Lourdes entered the church.

The altar had been destroyed, the pews flung apart. From a window a high light fell across the gallery and upon the apse wall. Just above, on the vault ceiling, a fresco.

Saint Sophia . . . The Mother Widow and her three haloed daughters: Pistis—Elpis—and Agape. Martyred women all. Time had phantomed the paints, leeching their shine, condemning their glory to everyday dust, yet never stealing the artist's soul. Not even the blood streaked across the women and meant as desecration had done that.

He thought of his own mother who had risen from unbearable sorrows. He thought of the heritage that had shaped and colored him, and he thought of the gentleman from the state department who had told him this assignment was given because he was not white. In the war between the flesh and faith, who will reign? How many times the old priest in El Paso had said that in answer to the everyday persecutions of life.

Outside the church a bell was suspended from a heavy yoke. John Lourdes reached up inside the open mouth to feel for the clapper. From far down the dirt road Hain called out, "Efendi, come! Bring your field glasses!"

⁓

THE BODIES LAY at the stony bottom of a hundred foot drop. Through his field glasses most looked to John Lourdes to have died from the fall. A small number, perhaps two dozen, had survived long enough to try and drag themselves to a stream, where beyond were woods. He could see the marks their bodies had made scoring the earth. A bare handful reached the water, those looked to have been shot.

"The men of the village?" said John Lourdes.

"It would seem so."

Crossing the town square John Lourdes said, "Get a rope and ring the bell." He opened one of the scabbards stored on the pack horse.

"There are Turks everywhere, efendi. There are Kurd bandits in these hills. The Pasha has opened the prisons of murderers and they ride for the government in armed battalions. Some are stationed at Erzurum not nine kilometers from here."

John Lourdes checked the pump action on his M12.

"If you ring the bell, efendi, someone will hear . . . someone will come."

"That's the goddamn idea." He chambered 20 gauge shells into the underbelly of the weapon. "Get a rope, attach the clapper, ring the bell. And keep ringing it. I was to meet the dragoman of the *vilayet* here. I've got to know if he's alive, if anyone from here is left alive who can tell me that."

"It's Malek. The priest. He is the journey."

John Lourdes swung a bandoleer of shells over his shoulder. "He is the journey."

———

THE RING CARRIED well into the hills, and when it died away Hain rang again. John Lourdes sat on the edge of the well in the town square with the shotgun across his lap and watched. When the right arm of the guide gave way, he switched to the left. And so it went. The mist had finally burned off, and the light fell hard upon the country. A country, John Lourdes thought, that seemed well provisioned with possibility. Then, in the watching, something about the horses gave him pause.

"Do you have a gun?" said John Lourdes.

"I have a revolver at my saddle."

"Get it. But keep it in a pocket."

Hain moved quickly. His head like a hummingbird scanning left and right.

"How do you know Mr. Baptiste?" said John Lourdes.

"Baptiste? He was my attorney once. He kept me out of prison.

He was a fine attorney, with but one failing. He was not corrupt. Efendi, is there something?"

"You're the guide."

They first came within sight by a stand of timber. Three riders approaching through the high grass at a slow walk. They maneuvered to keep the sun at their backs.

Hain was visibly shaken. He slipped the revolver under his grimy blouse.

They turned up into the street, this mismatched set of men led by an old one. They were not Kurds, nor bandits, not part of the murderers' battalion. They were Turkish soldiers.

Recognizing this the guide sprinted forward. He threw himself to the dirt in front of the horsemen. A tone of pleading and supplication in his voice, a dramatic gesturing of the arms punctuated a tortured monologue. John Lourdes did not need a dictionary to know he was being thrown to the dogs.

seven

HE OLD ONE stared at John Lourdes. He had a grim and tireless face. He addressed John Lourdes directly.

"This one," he said, gesturing at Hain, "tells you are a friend of the Armenian. And looking for the dragoman of the *vilayet*. That you tricked him to bring you here."

The old one, surprisingly, spoke a fair brand of English.

"Is this truthful?"

"Who is on the ground, and who is not."

The speaker addressed the two other riders quietly. As he did John Lourdes moved the barrel of the shotgun just slightly, for a better killing angle. The old one dismounted. Then, without ceremony, he kicked Hain full in the face.

"Are you," he now asked John Lourdes, "friend to the Armenian?"

"Wouldn't know one if I saw one."

"And the dragoman?"

"I am a citizen of Mexico. Here to see the country."

His questioner took a step toward John Lourdes and as he did the guide came up like a gun-shot djinn and got his arm around that aging throat pressing a black and heavy revolver into the man's stomach, all the while making this mad trill that shocked the soldiers' mounts so they skittered and turned. John Lourdes now was up and shotgun ready.

Hain shouted into the side of the old one's face, "The hind legs of the dog have risen."

The soldiers were uncertain and rattling out threats and demands. The old one put up a hand to quiet them then said directly to John Lourdes, "The letter Mr. Baptiste gave to a man . . . had a quote from the Book."

"Shoot them, efendi. Shoot them now."

John Lourdes threw out a hand, "Wait." He came forward and eased the gun barrel down just a bit. "You tell me? What Gospel . . . What chapter?"

"Luke," came the reply. "Chapter ten."

"Verses twenty-five to thirty-seven," said John Lourdes.

"The tale of the Samaritan."

John Lourdes let the gun barrel drop. He ordered the guide to do the same.

"I am the dragoman," said the old one and put out a hand.

They shook.

"Efendi," said John Lourdes, "I almost killed you."

"It is you who both were about to be killed."

He then motioned for John Lourdes to look over his shoulder. There, in the cool shadows of the church gallery was a boy with a musket.

A DRAGOMAN WAS an official functionary and, as John Lourdes could best piece together, a sort of trading post politico and interpreter serviceable in a host of Arabic and European languages.

The two soldiers with the dragoman were his sons, the younger boy with the relic firearm, his grandson. The Turkish uniforms they'd stripped from their victims were a means of moving more freely about the countryside, as they had become hunted men. No Armenian, John Lourdes learned, was allowed to carry weapons.

They sat about the well, they smoked and drank coffee heated in a battered can. John Lourdes asked about the priest, as was his mission. The dragoman had discouraging news. The priest had been captured in a battle along the Karusi River, which was at the headwaters of the Euphrates. He was now imprisoned at Erzurum. The tribunal's sentence was, of course, death. Yet, he was not to be afforded the mantle of martyrdom.

His fate—an insane asylum in Constantinople. There he was to be broken. He was to admit the Armenian was at the root of all trouble within the Ottoman Empire. To confess the Armenian had been, and was now, in consort with Europe and the Entente in trying to overthrow the legitimate government. That a free state financed by the industrial west was to be designed without the Muslim. And that the free state was to be paid for with the Dardanelles and the Persian Gulf. And with the prize of prizes—the oil fields of Basra and Baku. As the priest Malek had told the people, "The holy water of the future will come from the well of oil."

The dragoman and his sons meant to confront infamy. Theirs was a plot to free the priest. John Lourdes asked if he might know the plan, to lend reasonable advice, if he had such to offer. To that end, a ride to the prison at Erzurum must be undertaken.

ERZURUM STOOD UPON a flat plateau amidst a vast plain with nothing to hold back the wind. Where the sun was, sheer mountains rose tipped with snow. Erzurum had been at the crossroads of violence since wars with the Seleucids and Parthians.

Their small band passed through the shadow of the fortress gate and along a stone boulevard lined with trees. There were many soldiers and tourists and women wearing black chadors so that only their eyes were revealed. Above the rooftops were minarets glazed with tiles, and they shined like some striking image against the sun.

On a long dirt street were the bazaars where traders and cobblers sold their wares beside food merchants and goodsmen and jewelers of Oltu Tasi that had been carved into prayer beads and pipes and necklaces.

The dragoman and his sons were dressed now in common garb and rode quietly with their noses toward the ground. They put up their horses and dismounted, and John Lourdes and Hain followed them up a flight of stairs to a rooftop café. From their table they could look across the pavilion to the prison.

It was walled and grim, with a guard station and rifletower beside an iron gate. There was a courtyard framed by two stories of barred windows. In the empty dirt courtyard a man stood chained to a stake.

"Malek," said the dragoman.

He, alone, was there. On view to all in the prison, to all who walked past the gate. His clothes less than that of a beggar, he was left to urinate in the dust where he stood barefooted.

John Lourdes told his companions he would walk the street alone and survey the prison close at hand. He passed under the shadow of the tower, which fell long across the earth. The walls were of rough-cut stone as was the tower, and the gate iron was thick as the bone of a human thigh. The guards were indifferent to his passing, for many who went by the gate slowed in their curiosity over this chained likeness of a man.

Malek stood in the prison sun staring straight ahead. He gave the guards no notice, nor any to the shouts and calls of the prisoners from their cells, and none to the citizenry passing in the street. He was unto himself, alone in a place beyond question or reason.

He was not a tall man, nor a powerful man. Though his face hair was scored with gray and the earthy skin marred by lines, John Lourdes thought him to be about fifty, the same age as his father would be, had he lived.

It was only when Malek took a slow and awkward step to one side, as if to keep the blood coursing through his legs, that John Lourdes saw the priest's feet. Truly saw them. From the rooftop he had appeared barefooted. It was so. But there was something attached to the bottom of those naked soles. Something the color of iron, and when the priest put a foot down there was a discernable clunk, sending up a small bundle of dust.

Horseshoes. They were nailed to his feet. John Lourdes kept staring to make sure the evidence of his eyes was correct. And yet, there was nothing about the man, nothing in the way he stood or moved, to suggest such an atrocity had been inflicted upon him.

John Lourdes had seen men like this in the west. In the fenceless counties of Texas and Mexico. Men, usually older, but not always, who bled more, endured more, had been defeated more, suffered and survived more, yet whose very being seemed to support the flesh of the body on a scaffold of character and soul. Men, who even when exhausted beyond endurance, inhabited an unassailable place.

Such men could, and did, have tortured or flawed characters, they could be broken or destroyed. And though the universe is not in the business of the commonplace or the extravagant, the universe does not lie.

John Lourdes turned his attention to the layout of the courtyard, to the heavy wooden doors on the prison square, the forty yards or so of barren space between Malek and the gate. He assessed the guards' ability to command the scene, the weapons the men carried, how the gate locked and was hinged to the stone, the street as a means of defense and escape. He took out his notebook and began to draft his first ideas. Then, after a few moments writing, he stopped.

Four men, he thought, four men. He looked across the pavilion to where they watched him from the café. Four men, and one is old and one a boy.

As he crossed the pavilion, he noted a company of riders coming up through the bazaar. At the head of the column was Rittmeister Franke. John Lourdes quickly crossed inside the rippling cloth of a trader's tent.

The German was followed by brother officers and members of the Turkish Special Organization that had been with him on *Le Minotaur*. But the other men with him were not troops.

It was a commission of the foul and the wretched. Recruits from some dark nightmare with scythes across their shoulders and double headed axes protruding from scabbards. Some carried rifles and scimitars, and clubs fleshed with metal arrowtips. Their clothes bore the filth of the nation and this cast of horribles gave no man his due, nor expected any.

The guide came up behind John Lourdes and leaned into his shoulder. "The officers . . . They were on the same boat as you."

"Yes. Who are those others?"

"Remember, efendi, I spoke of murderers let out of the prisons if they would ride for the government. These are the ones released to hunt and kill the Armenian."

eight

NIGHT FELL ABOUT the prison. The barred windows left their image upon the walls. John Lourdes and the dragoman faced each other over a candle on the rooftop. The old one explained his plan. John Lourdes listened and smoked and considered. When done, the dragoman asked, "You have looked, you have heard. Now, tell me what you think."

From beyond a street of rooftops a muezzin made the evening call to prayer. The lilt of the words hung on the still air like silk. John Lourdes did not know what they meant, but the chant seemed plaintive and touched with the promises of faith.

He looked toward the prison. There was a great wheel of light above the tower roof made of lamps. It stood out across the city like a burning eye. He was able to watch the guards there taking their time of the *adhan*. In the darkness beyond the gate the priest waited on daylight.

"John Lourdes . . . What do you see?"

"Efendi, I see you are not enough."

"But, we are all there is."

John Lourdes acknowledged as much. The others around the candle spoke not at all. Except for the guide. He thumbed tobacco into his *chibouk* and asked in a pleasant tone if anyone had a miracle on them. If not, he would settle for a match.

THE NEXT DAY John Lourdes reenvisioned the plan.

He decided the moment for the assault to be the afternoon call to prayer. The night before, he noted that was when the tower guards were at their most vulnerable.

There were two avenues of escape from the pavilion. The street with its chaotic bazaar, and a smaller street, further down from the gate that cut into the pavilion at an angle. Out that cobbled pass-way is where they would make the run, if they survived the assault.

John Lourdes stationed the grandson at the corner of that street, as he could watch for the gendarmes or soldiers that might happen upon the scene, and he could provide support fire on the gate. At the corner the boy staked both his mount and one for the priest and squatted beside them. He took a Qur'an from his blouse. He was to be nothing more than a young man studying the book of divine guidance till it was time.

The dragoman's two sons took up positions against the pavilion wall that fronted the prison gate. They sat and played *tawula*, mindlessly rolling the dice and moving the checkers as the every-day business of life passed by. Between them were rolled up prayer rugs that hid carbines and an ax to break the priest's chains.

It had fallen to the dragoman to detonate the tower and gate.

John Lourdes asked how this was to be accomplished in broad daylight and within reach of the guard's spit. The old one then told him a story he had heard in the last few years, and he went about investigating if it were true, for he knew the Armenian and the Turk would eventually feast on the extermination of the other.

He learned that in 1905 a man named Jorris had improvised an explosive device using a vehicle and a clock-operated bomb. In July of that year, a group of Armenian separatists had attempted to assassinate the Caliph of the Faithful as he entered a mosque for Friday night prayers.

The dragoman told John Lourdes he had learned how to construct such a device. That they had a truck hidden away and ready to deliver the explosives. In its flatbed were piles of chain and pieces of pipe, along with stacks of odd fittings and shards of iron. All of which was covered with hay and waiting on the device and driver.

John Lourdes saw the flaw in the old one's plan and expressed his concern. The flaw being the dragoman. How could he park a truck beside the tower and gate without drawing attention to himself, if not outright suspicion? Would it not be reasonable for the Turkish guards to suspect him of being Armenian and a threat. What if they confronted him and searched the truck before the planned moment of detonation. And even if he held them at bay till the detonation, but was killed, the support for his sons' attempt at freeing the priest would be cut in half.

The dragoman had no answer. How could he? He was not short of mind, he was short of men.

John Lourdes decided it would be best for the dragoman to cover the gate from the entrance to the street of the bazaar. And to oversee an alternative route of escape laid out in that direction, on the misfortune it were necessary.

"Who then will drive the truck?" said the dragoman.

John Lourdes answered, "I will."

"Have you experience driving a truck?"

Of all the questions, thought John Lourdes, he could have asked. "I've driven some," he said.

<hr />

THE DAY WAS windless and clear as John Lourdes downshifted up the plateau road and through the city gate. Erzurum was in a high state of alarm after a series of reports from the news organizations. There were soldiers everywhere. Advance scouts of the Russian army had been spotted by a reconnaissance balloon east of Van, a hundred kilometers from Erzurum. An attack against that city was imminent within the month.

In the Armenian quarter of Van the citizens were illegally arming themselves for a stand against the Turkish troops stationed there, hoping then to join forces with an Allied assault. In the streets of Erzurum people spoke of the Armenian as a traitor that should be treated no better than tainted meat.

The truck turned into that street of tents and trading stalls inching through a confusion of human traffic that cursed the truck or slammed their fists on the engine hood at its very presence.

On the front seat between John Lourdes and the dragoman and hidden under a span of cloth were the explosives and timer. John Lourdes noticed his passenger glance at the seat then look away. It would be a few more minutes yet.

"I would like to see your country one day," said the dragoman.

"Yes?"

"The movies. I get to see the cities and the people. The customs. The hats. I love the hats."

The old one smiled, as did John Lourdes.

Yards later, through the tents and traffic they could see where the street opened into the pavilion, and the prison.

"John Lourdes?"

"Yes."

"Have you seen war?"

"I have seen war."

The dragoman lifted the cloth and spread it across his lap. He placed the device on the cloth. John Lourdes glanced at him as he readied the clock, checked again the wires, set the timer. The fingers were long and thin and deeply wrinkled, but very assured. The dragoman folded the cloth back over the device. His face rose, his eyes fixed on the way ahead.

The truck was barely moving as the dragoman stepped out. People squeezed past, Arab and European alike. The noise was overwhelming. He slipped the device far into the hay that covered the flatbed. He quickly went back to the truck door. He looked in the window. "Five minutes," he told John Lourdes. "The call to prayer will begin very soon . . . Five minutes."

With that, he stepped away and pressed on through the crowd toward the pavilion, where he disappeared.

As the truck labored past the last tents John Lourdes scanned the pavilion to make sure everyone was in position. Hain was near the café, watching over their mounts with the dragoman walking towards him. As they were setting off that morning he'd told John Lourdes, "I will serve you better than a brave man . . . or a man of beliefs."

"Let's just hope all that money you bartered for won't weigh you down too much."

Before he walked off John Lourdes caught him by the arm. He spoke so the others could not hear. "In the pavilion . . . if anyone is wounded and cannot go on . . . you're to make sure there's nothing left to be interrogated."

John Lourdes drove across the pavilion and eased the truck toward the prison till he had it cradled up alongside the tower. He turned off the rig and got out. He had a piece of paper in his hand and was studying it as if something was written there.

He could see the black image of the tower in the pavilion dust and the movement of a man with a rifle along its railing. A voice in Turkish called out loudly. John Lourdes kept his attention on the paper, walking what seemed aimlessly, turning finally, acknowledging ultimately the guard who was pointing with the rifle at the truck, motioning to move it. Another guard came out of the gate shack and stood by the iron bars. Before long he was joined by yet still another guard.

John Lourdes tried to explain in Spanish, but it was futile and finally holding up the piece of paper stumbled out a few words, "Ben . . . ah . . . kayip. Kayip?"

The guards didn't give a damn about him being lost. The sweep of their gestures and tone of their demands meant they wanted the truck gone. John Lourdes offered an apologetic half bow and said, "Yardim etmek." He was pointing somewhere vaguely across the pavilion. "Yardim etmek."

He walked toward the horses and, looking back, saw a collection of soldiers doubletiming it across the courtyard and past the priest to the prison gate. Then came the first call of the adhan. The rising pitch of the voice carrying across the pavilion.

For a moment the guards were more vested in their faith than in the truck. John Lourdes watched the dragoman walk his mount toward the street of the bazaar, and it was then he heard the guide. He was calling out, "Efendi! The café roof!" There, the two German officers under Rittmeister Franke were looking down into the pavilion, staring oddly at John Lourdes, who had reached the horses.

Field glasses hung from the Arab's saddlehorn. John Lourdes took them and slipped the loop over his neck. He did the same with a satchel of ammunition. From one scabbard he took an Enfield and worked his shoulder through its strap. From the other he took the M12.

He turned. Hain was calling to him ever more desperately. One officer was part way down the roof stairs, the other was crossing the pavilion. On that clear and windless day there could be not more than a minute, a minute at the very most, before this small patch of universe tasted pure death.

Time slowed for John Lourdes to a near standstill. A fine dust drifted across the pavilion in a near drowsy fashion. Figures moving through the sunlight along the prison wall were like snapshots imprinted upon the day. John Lourdes seemed suddenly possessed by a strange and unearthly calm. A veiled woman passed before him, her eyes fixed upon the foreign creature carrying so much weaponry. Others he passed also stared, their faces anchored to his presence. It was as if the din across that pavilion had died away, and all he was left with was the sound of the gravel crunching beneath his boots.

"Efendi . . ." Hain was shouting from behind him. ". . . Efendi!"

John Lourdes, without looking, ordered, "Kill him."

He did not see the guide fire, nor the German officer collapse to his knees.

John Lourdes chambered a shell into his M12. People were running. Escaping the pavilion. A couple, European, the woman carrying a parasol and in all those ruffles, trying to run from the inevitable—

nine

THE STONE WALLS of that prison may have been hallowed for withstanding centuries of the broadsword and spear, but they did not belong to the province of the future. The sheer ferocity of the explosion lifted the truck as high as the tower and bits of wall and iron fittings fell across rooftops streets away. Bodies were flung far into the pavilion, pockets of smoke rose from their uniforms where scraps of metal had scored a pathway to the bone.

The guard tower was consumed in fire, and from this ancient battlement smoke billowed skyward into the still air ever blackening, ever thickening. The gate had been blown into the courtyard, uprooting the post where the priest had been chained. He now lay beneath this bent monstrosity alive but unable to shoulder the weight and free himself.

The brothers plunged past the burning wreckage upended beside the gate. Part of the tower had collapsed across the entry. The guard shack was in ruin, a gaping hole in the prison wall next to it. The courtyard clouded with smoke. As the brothers scaled the debris John Lourdes took up a position at the gate, where he could command the courtyard and the pavilion.

The few guards left were scattered amidst the rubble. One staggered blindly toward the barracks. Through the haze John Lourdes could hear carbine fire killing them where they lay, while across the pavilion the guide was in a running gunfight with the surviving officer.

The grandson rode headlong toward the gate with the priest's mount. Great shocks of flame erupting up through the truck windshield and chassis caused the horses to veer wildly. The German officer had taken something from his saddle wallet, and John Lourdes intuitively knew. "Kill him now!" he shouted to the guide. "You've got to kill him now—"

The officer's horse was felled by a shot and the great chest swung about and the whole of its weight collapsed upon him but not before the officer fired off a signal flare. It tailed across the pavilion and burst above the prison and a starfield burned then fell through the waves of smoke.

John Lourdes leapt fallen tower stones and entered the courtyard. The prisoners were shrieking at the bloodshed. Their arms stretching through the window bars, their faces in the dusty air all wild and frenetic. The brothers had the gate near lifted. One shouldered it on his back while the other helped the priest pull free from beneath it.

A barracks door was thrown open, guards came charging out into the courtyard. John Lourdes turned his shotgun on them and the door wood splintered, and the wall stone nicked, and there was blood on the wall and blood on the wood and pockets of it in the dust that followed the scattering trail of the wounded. There were empty shell casing all about John Lourdes' boots and the prisoners wailed with vengeful joy at the carnage.

A guard leaned out from the roof and shot the brother holding up the gate. He tried to gasp air in past the breach in his throat as John Lourdes chambered round after round till the guard reeled away from the ledge holding the front of his uniform which was a bloodmask of holes.

As the brother crumpled to the ground, John Lourdes rushed over and braced up that mass of iron using his shotgun as a crossbar. He held long enough for the priest to get dragged free.

The dragoman now reached the guard tower. John Lourdes shouted to him for cover fire while they got the priest out. The guide came riding toward them with the rest of the mounts. John Lourdes let the gate fall and helped the priest stand. He yelled to Hain to come on. The guide jumped to the ground and ordered the dragoman to keep rein on the horses. With gun drawn he vaulted the burning truck and was gone into the clouded gray of the courtyard.

It was a scene of pandemonium with guards striking out of the smoke and along the roof and the prisoners howling up vile degradations and rattling clay bowls and wooden spoons across the bars. John Lourdes swung the empty shotgun onto one shoulder and took the Enfield from the other and put up a wall of fire. Retreating backwards toward the gate over the bodies of the slain he and the guide left a trail of stripper clips and shell casings and the dust they trampled through was wet with red that clung to their boots and the bottom of their trouser legs.

Between the smoke and fire the horses reared and shied but they managed to lift the chained and hobbled priest up on a mount. He braced the withers with his legs and shook his head he would be all right. Once they were all mounted and clustered up by the burning wreckage of that fallen gate, John Lourdes gave the order.

They started across the empty pavilion. People huddled up in doorways and stairwells watching the nightmare of a gunbattle. When they reached the far street the riders had to pull up. A platoon was coming toward them at a trot. They spotted the heavily armed riders streaked with dust and the priest in chains and they formed up along the road and began a volley fire.

The riders wheeled about, retreating into a wall of dust of their own making. When they raced past the tower a guard stepped from the yawing flames and fired into their ranks.

There was a cry as the remaining brother was driven from the saddle. His foot caught in the stirrup and he was dragged under the mount. Its spindly legs tripped over him and the horse flipped, and it and the rider lay dead in the shadow of the prison wall.

The dragoman now led them through the abandoned bazaar where the horses sidestepped carts and jumped crates as the riders tore with their arms at tents in their path.

They turned into a bare street awash with light. They could hear the clatter of hooves on stone at a run. They turned down into a walled avenue to be stared at in disbelief as they commanded and whipped with the reins for a path to be cleared.

The street opened into a square that troops were crossing at a full gallop toward the prison. They were forced back the way they came and at the next crossing were met head on by two mounted Turkish soldiers.

The shadows of pursuers and pursued overlapped as they fired into each other. The priest charged the soldiers whipping at them with the chains that bound him. In the confusion the troops retreated. The fight grew more intense and wild at close range. The grandson was gutshot, the horse the old one rode toppled and he was flung into a wall. The chain the priest wielded tore across the soldier's eyes and momentarily blinded him. John Lourdes brought the Enfield to bear. One soldier was taken in the saddle and his mount bolted away with him slouching there lifelessly; the other was wounded and fell to the street and was killed under the hooves of the riders.

They circled up with people scattering before them. John Lourdes swung out of the stirrups and knelt over the dragoman. His left wrist was broken and he was dazed and beyond riding and the grandson began to sag out of the saddle and it was the priest who sided him and held the boy to keep him from collapsing into the street. The boy was holding his stomach and there was blood seeping through the youth's fingers.

"Efendi . . ." The guide's mount reared back on its hindquarters. "We must go."

The dragoman understood and addressed the priest in Armenian, asking he leave, and he told John Lourdes. "I said to go. Take the priest and—"

The priest answered. It was the first John Lourdes heard the voice. It was gruff and deeply emotional, and the priest regarded John Lourdes with a stare that breathed authority and will.

"Efendi," said the guide. "The fool won't go."

"I can see that."

John Lourdes stood and surveyed the wreckage that was these men. He wiped the sweat and dust from his eyes. This small patch of ground at that moment was the universe. He looked there for the answer, searched there for the answer, hoped there somewhere, somewhere, an answer—

He moved toward Hain. He pointed, "The *araba*."

The guide swung about. Sitting in a dusty lot between hovels was an old and heavy coach of faded black drawn by two horses drinking from a wooden trough.

"Get it!" said John Lourdes.

The guide kicked his mount and sped off. John Lourdes swung the Enfield up on his free shoulder and helped the dragoman to his feet.

Hard wheels were trundling toward them with Hain at the whip. People along the street stood frozen in amazement or anger. A man leaned out a second-story window thick faced and furious and pointing at the rig.

As the guide pulled to a stop he yelled, "Efendi, it seems we have made yet another enemy!"

The *araba* was a converted hackney. Four wheels, black cloth for windows. The wheels had been painted red and there were long plumes of colored feathers at the four posts of the coach roof. It was a ridiculous looking affair if ever there was one. And as was the custom, the seats had been pulled out and passengers either sat or lay about on cushions.

John Lourdes walked the dragoman to the coach steps and was turning to help with the boy, but the priest had already dismounted and was carrying the badly wounded youth in his arms.

There he was, in chains and with those pieces of iron hammered into his soles and scarcely able to lift a foot, and yet he was carrying the boy. Carrying the boy and climbing into the wagon, mute to his own suffering.

He turned to John Lourdes and spoke. John Lourdes looked to the guide who translated, "The priest said, 'thank you . . . for the boy.'"

ten

THEY HAD CLOSED the carriage's dark shades and the guide pushed those drafthorses hard through the streets with John Lourdes following. The *araba* bounced and shook and sometimes skidded and the long roof feathers pricked back like the windfashioned plumage on a lady's bonnet. When the rig turned into a dirt street that descended a long hill the guide put out a hand that he was slowing and for John Lourdes to see ahead.

Fronting the street below was a *madrese*—the Cifte Minareli— named for its two minarets. There troops bivouacked on the road beside the great school.

The daylight was going, the *madrese* walls of dark volcanic tufa now stood in their own shadow. John Lourdes eased his mount up to flank the coach. The soldiers' attention was on a distant part of the city where a lake of smoke spread across the windless blue.

John Lourdes looked back, watching vigilantly. On the crest of the hill face they were just descending was a column of riders. It was Rittmeister Franke and that army of convicts. They were moving along the boulevard with a steady resolve. There was a glare at the head of the column. Shiny, mirror-like. John Lourdes understood: the captain was searching with field glasses.

The guide spoke, "Efendi?"

"I know," said John Lourdes. "We have even less ammunition than we've had luck."

AT THE *MADRESE* John Lourdes chose not to follow the *araba*. He had come to a decision, a gamble really, which he explained to the guide and those in the coach.

He, alone, went along the avenue that bordered the base of the hill where Rittmeister Franke and the men with him rode. He placed himself out in the open, to insure that if the captain knew who he was hunting, it was only John Lourdes that would be found.

He glanced back at the *araba*. It was making its way past all those troops, in the same manner as all the other carriages. Hain was casual and courtly to those he passed. And then, in a moment that was purely brazen, the guide stood up in the seat and called to the troops, shouting that he was praying for the swift destruction of an enemy too ignominious to name. That chancy little bastard, thought John Lourdes.

He watched the *araba* till it was long down the street and clear of danger. He had put rifle and shotgun back in their scabbard. The satchel with the ammunition was looped to the saddle. He took the glasses that hung from his neck and focused in on the road above.

The column was still on the move. Officers could be seen galloping back from their search of side streets and alleys. As John Lourdes panned the roadway, Rittmeister Franke finally posted up in the lenses. He sat atop his mount. He was scanning the city below. He was extraordinarily meticulous. He would stay fixed on a place for a long while then the field glasses would meter slightly.

John Lourdes waited and watched. In due course the captain came to bear upon that place in the road where John Lourdes sat atop the Arabian in the last runs of daylight. The captain's gaze fixed, he leaned forward in the saddle. His cheeks and jaw white against the sun.

You're not sure of what you see, or are you, captain?

Through their field glasses each man was just a pistol shot removed from the other, and the movement of their mouths imminently visible.

Are you thinking . . . that's the citizen of Mexico down there. The one you told on the dock the other morning . . . there would come a time . . . when with your help . . . my rightful country would belong to me. You thinking about that moment now? My rightful country. It may come to pass. And if it does . . . it will mean something different than you ever dreamed.

Another officer rode up to Rittmeister Franke. It was the German who had sent up the flare.

You survived, Lieutenant. You should have taken your rightful place among the dead. Well . . . dust yourself off, there's always tomorrow.

The lieutenant took the field glasses from his saddle wallet and began to scan the roads below. But the captain—

That's right. Spend a little time reflecting. Cause the longer you keep your stare on me, the further those who mean to stand against you are stealing away . . . in, of all things, a half-assed coach with bird feathers.

73

Men from that crew of murderers now rode into view, the ones with rifles. They dismounted and began to sight up John Lourdes. However accomplished they were as murderers and torturers and rapists, they left much to be desired as marksmen.

In a flash of contempt John Lourdes doffed his hat to the captain. By the time the crack of riflefire rolled across the avenue, John Lourdes was well beyond its reach and disappeared into the streets and alleys of that ageless world.

THERE WAS AN ancient clocktower at the southeast corner of the citadel. It was known as the Tepsi Minare. It had served the Ottomans as an observation tower during the Middle Ages for its commanding view of the plain.

The dragoman told John Lourdes to use the minare as a site marker. And with his compass travel from it due east a few kilometers to a road where a stone bridge crossed a shallow river. There, those who survived would meet.

At sunset John Lourdes waited at the bridge and smoked as the clay-colored waters passed over the stream rocks beneath him. He was too wary and worried to rest.

He heard the turn of the wheels along the battered road and the slow cadence of harness metal before the black *araba* with its strange plumage appeared out of the last of a fired sky. Throwing away his cigarette he followed the coach over the bridge and off the road into a shadowy world of trees.

The grandson was still alive. They lay him upon the ground and Hain took a cushion from the coach for the boy to rest his head upon. The grandson knew that death was near as did his grandfather and the priest. The boy was not afraid to die, but what weighed most upon his heart was the need to know that he had served well.

He needed to hear the words, to take them into his weakening body, so that he might wear the beauty of them when he entered the garden of forever.

The grandfather and the priest knelt beside the child, for that is all he truly was, while John Lourdes and the guide kept back. What they knew, as the grandfather took a pistol from his waist-belt, was that dying boy could not be left behind. That with daylight they must travel hard and that the grandson's bones would be along a nameless riverbank by a bridge near the citadel of Erzurum for eternity.

The boy's eyes were closed, and the gun in the grandfather's hand trembled at the thought of the act he was to commit, while his broken wrist hung down painfully.

The guide whispered to John Lourdes, "The old man can't put the powder to him," and John Lourdes' look told him to shut his mouth.

John Lourdes could not take his eyes from the dragoman and the grandson. The old one had awoken that morning and he and his blood and the blood of his blood had set out upon a journey. And before this night would close he would be all that was left. He alone would carry daylight to a farther place.

I know this moment, thought John Lourdes, *it is with me always. It is as close as right now and as distant as any distant days I could imagine. I carry it in the same place we attribute to God. And it bears my father's name.*

It was the priest who took the weapon from the old one and it was he who cradled the boy's head in his arms so that their faces and spirits were near as one. It was the priest who ordered the guide to bring water, and the priest put out a scarred hand and with the water poured there went about a final blessing, touching the child's forehead and lips.

As he did he told this child that he had earned with his heart and courage a place in the tent of the father of all nations, from the Palestine to the Persian Sea. And that this tent was open on all sides, to all travelers, and that all travelers would know him, for he was a part of all travelers. And that the waters he drank there, and the waters he gave others to drink there were the waters of immortality. And that his face would be part of the face that saw us all before we were. And that he would be the one waiting to tell those who had been refused food and the shelter of caverns and who had been put under the dark waters that a doubtful world would be a thing of memory, to be forgotten by divine favor. And that his grandfather was proud of him, as the priest was proud of him. And the priest loved him as the grandfather loved him. And the priest hoped one day to be worthy of the sacrifice the child had made, and then the priest put his own hand around the child's and the grandfather put his hand around them both and in that moment so fleeting and eternal, the priest fired.

eleven

RIEF WAS A luxury they could not afford.

The guide dug a meager grave with his knife while John Lourdes made a splint and braced up the dragoman's wrist and hand. When they loosed the priest from his chains, Malek labored to the *araba* and sat with his back against a wheel. He slipped his arms through the spokes and then he called to the guide. It was time to get the iron shoes that had been hammered into the soles of his feet pried loose.

Hain looked at John Lourdes. "I can't do it," he said.

"I don't understand."

The guide could not look at John Lourdes, he could not look at the priest, who kept questioning him. He would not explain himself. Always nervous, his eyes were even more fugitive than usual. It wasn't fear, John Lourdes saw that. It was something else.

"Heat a knife," said John Lourdes, "to cauterize the wound. Tear strips of cloth from one of the cushions."

"Yes, efendi."

John Lourdes undid his vest, he removed his shirt. He placed them on the ground by his hat. He went to the stream. He washed the dust and blood from his hands. He ran palmfuls of water over his head and down his face. He returned to the fire and was given the cloth, which he bound around his hands to keep a firm grip, for he knew the feet would bleed much.

Malek was watching all the while. Through fire shadows he caught sight of the thick, hard scar from a bullet beneath John Lourdes' heart. He spoke.

"He wants to know," said the dragoman, "where you're from. I told him the United States."

"United States," said the priest. He shook his head sadly. He spoke then began to laugh.

"What?" said John Lourdes.

"The United States," said Hain. "To the priest, it isn't much, you see. It isn't England, to be sure. Nor France, for that matter. It is not even China. We are, after all, where we are from."

"I see," said John Lourdes. "Where is the mighty priest from?"

"He is Armenian," said the dragoman. "But he was born in Russia."

"And everyone knows Russia," said the guide. "The United States is not Russia."

John Lourdes squatted in front of the priest. They were eye-to-eye.

"He comes from Moscow," said the dragoman.

"And everyone knows Moscow," added Hain.

Malek asked another question.

"He wants to know where in the United States," said the dragoman.

"Tell him," urged the guide. "Maybe that will impress him."

John Lourdes cocked his head at an angle. "Texas," he said.

"Texas," repeated the dragoman.

"Ahhh, yes, Texas," said Hain, as if he knew the place intimately.

"He never heard of it," said the dragoman.

"Not even once," said the guide.

The priest took to repeating, "Tigziz . . . Tigziz." His tone was defamatory. He asked another question.

"He wants to know what Texas is like," said the dragoman.

"Yes, he wants to know," repeated the guide.

John Lourdes rubbed his chin with the back of a clothbound hand. "Tell him it's Russia . . . with balls."

The guide, of all people, said, "He's a priest."

"I don't give a damn if he's nephew to Jesus Christ. Tell him."

The dragoman told him.

The priest listened, the priest heard. The priest looked at John Lourdes with a stare that would melt iron. Then he laughed. "Tigziz . . . Tigziz." There was still derision in his tone, but as he continued, he stretched out one foot toward John Lourdes.

John Lourdes stared at the foot and realized. The priest had been prodding him, preparing him for what had to be done. Those iron shoes nailed into bone. A half measure was no measure at all. There would be blood, and there would be pain, and it would demand as much of one as it would the other.

⁓

THEY KILLED THE fire and slept, all except John Lourdes. He sat alone, away from the others, and smoked. There were tiny shapes of light in the nameless distance that he watched. A sudden hand on his shoulder startled him.

It was the priest.

In his own language he said that he, too, could not sleep. He squatted beside John Lourdes, who pointed to where he had been watching. The priest studied the curious tips of flame. They seemed to have a life of their own.

"Turks," said the priest.

"Or the Germans," said John Lourdes. "Rittmeister . . . cavalry."

He smoked. He glanced at the priest. The only sound the stream water running over rocks, that and both men's breathing. Malek seemed intensely preoccupied.

The priest then asked John Lourdes for a cigarette. He mimed smoking. John Lourdes took a beat to hell pack from his vest pocket. He lit it for the priest, who cupped his hands around the flame, to keep the wind from having at it. The priest inhaled generously.

"Father . . . you've got some hard fucking bark on you," said John Lourdes. "And it's a good thing. 'Cause Van is over a hundred kilometers from here and we need mounts."

WHERE THE PLAIN funneled into the rural foothills, the Turks had established a lookout post. It was strategically situated on a table of rock well above the roadway. A woeful shelter of mud and timber had been framed to the stone, and a stairwell of poor slat led to a covered scout post on the roof. Half a dozen mounted guards and one officer were stationed there. The poorly outfitted troops went about their lazy hours until the roof scout let out a warning. The men poured through the single doorway gathering up their weapons. Coming out of the landscape was an *araba*, the horses straining against the leads, dust rising wildly from the wheels. The driver stood in the seat pointing at a rider in a strange hat who was mounted on an Arabian and firing down upon that rattly coach as he lay chase.

The driver took to waving a white blouse. The guards were clustered around the shelter as the coach drew up. The horses were lathered and covered with dust.

From the driver's seat the guide called down to the guards that the pursuer was in the agency of the Triple Entente and in the *araba* was a captured Armenian traitor who had escaped from the prison at Erzurum.

The guide leapt to the ground. Scrambling past the guards, begging and bowing they please follow and see he swung the coach door open. He pulled the priest out and flung him to the ground.

"I captured him from—"

The guide then drew their attention to the rider. He had fallen back, and in fact, he had halted his pursuit altogether and was firing now at the coach from long range.

As the sergeant began to troop up his men to take control of the situation, a searing hole was blown through the black cloth drape that covered a coach window. Reeling backwards with arms outflung the sergeant landed dead there in the road.

For a moment the soldiers did not understand what happened or where the shot came from. From his hidden post inside the rig John Lourdes opened fire with the shotgun. The soldiers were immediately routed. They scattered up toward the shelter and the corral. The guide with his revolver lay chase. John Lourdes charged out from the far side of the coach. He shot over the pull horses and they took off in a panic and the *araba* went rumbling up on toward the foothills. The two men cut the soldiers down where they ran.

There followed a quick and leveling silence, but for the horses in the corral where they milled and whinnied nervously. It grew so quiet as the dust settled they could hear the slight thud of the hooves on hard ground and the creak of the corral posts where the horses pressed against them.

John Lourdes and the guide moved among the dead prodding at them with boot or slipper. The dragoman rode up on John Lourdes' mount, wearing John Lourdes' hat and carrying John Lourdes' rifle in his good hand. The priest stood.

John Lourdes instructed Hain, "In the shelter. Supplies . . . ammunition. Everything worth carrying."

Starting up toward the shelter the guide spoke. "Let's hope these were filthy drunks like most Turks."

The dragoman walked the Arabian to John Lourdes; he handed him back his hat.

"The corral," said John Lourdes. "Pick the best mounts. Weapons . . . If you see anything worth taking—"

The priest had not joined them. Something had his complete attention. He was kneeling over the sergeant's body. His companions stopped to watch. Malek rose. The sergeant's holster hung from his hand. He held it aloft so all could see. Dangling from the belt were prayer beads, necklaces, trinkets, cameos with pictures of family members and loved ones, rosaries of different colors, crucifixes. How many, who knows. The belt was thick with them.

Raising the holster against the sun there came this tinkle of gold and stone, glass and silver, like the voices of tiny birds.

John Lourdes understood. "Trophies," he said.

"Yes." answered the dragoman.

The priest lowered the holster. He ran a hand over the sergeant's Mauser and checked the weapon in a slow and careful manner. Then, he swung the belt around the back of his filthy robe and buckled it at the waist.

twelve

HERE WAS A sudden gunshot.

The guide lay flat on ground, smoke drifted up from his revolver. He shouted to the others. "There's a Turk still alive!"

He approached the shelter crawling on his belly, avoiding the window and door. The soldier was ordered to throw out his weapon and surrender.

A Mauser was tossed from the dark and landed in the dirt with a thud. Then, with hands raised, a figure appeared in the doorway. Sorry faced and scared. Twenty, maybe.

Hain scrambled to his feet, got hold of the soldier and shook him. "An officer no less. A lieutenant."

He asked the boy if he was in command, and the boy said he was, and the guide grunted. "Efendi . . . you know how someone this young gets to command in the Turkish army? Patronage . . . or . . .

he gave the commandant his ass." He hit the boy hard on the back with his weapon. "Which is it?"

"What do we do with him?" said the dragoman.

John Lourdes looked at the old one, then at the priest. The priest told the guide to bring the boy to him.

The guide kept hitting the lieutenant across the back of his neck and head with the butt of his revolver, prodding him forward. He asked the lieutenant how old he was, and the officer said, "Twenty." The guide then whispered, "You are going to be twenty forever." He gave a brutish kick to the back of the lieutenant's legs that forced him to his knees before the priest.

"Do you know who I am?"

The lieutenant did not look up.

"Do you know who I am?" repeated the priest.

He shook his head no.

"If you don't look at me, then how do you know?"

John Lourdes did not understand what was being said but as the officer looked up, he saw a young face that was broken with fear.

"Have you ever been to Erzurum?"

"Yes."

"Have you ever been to the prison there?"

"Yes."

Hain, who had been standing beside John Lourdes, suddenly turned and took off up the steps back toward the shelter. The priest, with the back of his fingers, began to strum the remains of a people that hung from the gunbelt.

"Have you ever been through the prison yard? What they call the courtyard?"

Silence.

"I will not ask you again."

The lieutenant's eyes went to the gunbelt where the priest's fingers kept strumming.

"Why are you looking at my hand?"

"I don't know—"

"You look, but you don't know why?"

"I—"

The priest now slipped his fingers under that long stream of prayer beads and necklaces so they rested there in his palm.

"Do you know what these are?"

Silence, but for the wind blowing dust along the road.

"Don't make me ask you again."

"I know what they are."

"What do you know about the man in the prison yard?"

"The priest?"

"The one they call Malek."

"They chain him to a stake."

"And what else?"

The lieutenant's eyes darted left, then right, and then as if by some power beyond reason or control, the eyes came to fall upon the priest's feet, bound up in bloody cloth.

"Why are you looking there?"

"The blood."

"But there is so much other blood to look at."

Malek waved an arm toward the sergeant lying in the road, his open eyes white against the bloody rag that was the face he would wear into eternity. At that moment the guide returned from the shelter. John Lourdes saw an ax rested on one shoulder.

"What have you done?" said the priest to the lieutenant.

"I've done nothing."

"What good is a soldier who does nothing?"

The lieutenant looked up at the priest, his was a profound con-fusion. "I didn't mean—"

"Then you have done something."

The ax landed in the dirt between the two men. The priest stared at the guide. The priest bent and took up the ax. The guide squatted on a rock close at hand to watch.

"What have you done?" said the priest again.

The lieutenant blinked repeatedly, his expression grew more confounded.

"You don't know how to answer to save your life," he said. "The Armenian women and children are told they are to be deported. If they refuse, they are killed. If they go, they are taken to the desert to be starved and butchered. Or brought to the sea and drowned. The men are told they are not allowed to bear arms. If they obey, they are helpless against the threat that means to take them. If they disobey, they are hunted and killed as enemies of the state. How are they to answer? How does anyone answer to save their life, when there is no answer that will save the life? Can you answer me that, soldier?"

The rising tide of anger in the priest John Lourdes saw was touched also with agony. The voice remained under control, the words premeditated. He touched the gunbelt. He ran his fingers along the hanging line of lives. "Were any of these taken by you?" he said.

"No . . . no."

"How do I know if you lie?"

"I have always been a truthful—"

"How do I know you won't swear to anything to save your life at this moment?"

"I—"

"Ahhh. I will tell you a story. About a man and a woman. My sister and her husband. I had in my possession two photographs of them. Until the gendarmes arrested me. They burned them in my presence. One was a picture of their wedding. The other was taken at a park in Erzurum in 1905 by a man of the newspapers. In that photograph they were lying dead with other Armenians. Four hundred. Lined up like fish. Struck down by a maelstrom of political force. The two photographs. The alpha and the omega."

The lieutenant's eyes went to each of the four men. The guide, squatting on that rock, kept pointing to the dead sergeant, pointing and nodding his head.

"My sister and her husband had two children," said the priest. "Gone to where? Who knows? Who looks out for them now . . . Who knows? Who knows even if . . . Who knows?" He took a long sad breath, "Now . . . I am left to hunt for them in my dreams."

John Lourdes did not understand a word but as he watched the face of the priest in the telling, it was a face he had seen and remembered from the Spanish books of God, with their illustrations of saints and demons and prophets in moments of unbridled fury. Then the priest brought the ax down.

It cut into a rock beside the lieutenant's head. The rock was larger than a man's fist and the ax blade struck with such force the stone was cleaved clear through, and the handle sheared in half.

The lieutenant clung to the earth downfaced and foundering until the priest reached and lifted him like a cloth doll. He then dragged off the Turk past John Lourdes a dozen or so paces. He held the boy's head in his powerful hands and whispered to him. Tears ran down the lieutenant's moon face. He was shaking shamelessly, and he nodded again and again at what the priest told him, and then the priest reached down to his waist and tore from the gunbelt a necklace. He held it up in front of the soldier's face and then forced it into his shirt and, with that, he shoved him into the road.

The Turk stumbled there, unsure, and then he started away, wiping at the tears and looking back in dread constantly. He then began to run.

The dragoman, who had been close enough to the priest and the boy to hear what was said, walked up to Malek. The priest was trembling with rage and he looked at his hands as if they were treacherous strangers with a life of their own. He and the dragoman spoke together, and then the priest turned and started away. He walked past John Lourdes with neither a word nor a look, and on up that foothill road that was to take them to Van.

thirteen

HEN THEY RODE on into the frontier they were well outfitted. They had two extra mounts weighted down with ammunition, food, ouzo, wine, and charcoal for a heavy brass samovar that clanged mercilessly as they made their way along trails footed for goats. They also now had, in John Lourdes' possession, a pouch he'd discovered in the shelter that carried letters and dispatches. It appears one of the dead was an envoy en route to Van by order of the *mutasarrif*—the district governor.

They rode single file above the valley floor through the cool blue shade of the afternoon, the guide in the lead. He looked back and spoke to John Lourdes, who rode behind him.

"Malek did that fool boy no favor. He cannot explain to his commanding officer how it came to be he is alive." Hain shook his head and laughed cynically. "The priest gave the boy a set of iron wings and asked him to fly."

John Lourdes glanced at the others following silently at a distance. "Did you hear what was said to him?"

"No, efendi, but I asked the old man."

"What did he say?"

"He called me the hind legs of the dog."

Darkness overtook them. They camped in the stone mountains. The guide filled the samovar with charcoal and they drank hot tea. John Lourdes sat near the fire with the dragoman who read through the documents and translated while John Lourdes wrote in his notebook anything he thought of import or value.

He would occasionally glance across the flames to where Malek sat alone. He had the gunbelt off and was studying each memento with deliberate intimacy. John Lourdes came to realize the priest was praying over each.

John Lourdes said to the dragoman, "I'd like to ask you something."

"What the priest said to the lieutenant?"

"Yes."

The dragoman looked toward the guide. "That one asked before. He said you wanted to know. Of course, I saw he was lying."

"In my country they say, there are people who will lie even when the truth sounds better."

The dragoman nodded in agreement.

The guide was squatting beside the samovar. He was adding ouzo to his tea and smoking his *chibouk*. His face moved nervously in some world of lost thoughts, but when he saw he was being stared at he grinned.

"As to your earlier question," said the dragoman.

"If you can't tell me—"

"No. I can tell you. It has been on my mind all day." He paused, then said, "He told the soldier that if he wanted to live he must make a promise."

"And the promise?"

"That after the war if, god willing, he were alive, he was to take an orphan child into his home and raise the child in the Armenian faith and tradition."

The deeper implications of this were not difficult for John Lourdes to understand, for they cut to the raw core of every conflict. "That's why he put the necklace down his shirt."

"Yes, that is right."

"I'm sure you asked, but how does he know that fellow will keep the promise."

"Of course. Tell me . . . what would you say?"

John Lourdes considered, "He had no answer," he said. "For you cannot answer a question there is no answer to."

"You listen well. Yet, Malek also told him . . . 'We are in a war. But, at the end of the war, any war, all wars, there is no way of knowing what kind of peace a man, any man, every man, will have to make with himself, as well as with others.'"

WHEN THEY MOUNTED up that morning it was gray with only a rumor of light. The wind blew their tracks away as quickly as the horses made them. Beyond the mountain line a low tremor of thunder, and the air soon smelled of rain.

They approached a large village at the base of a volcanic monolith that looked to be chiseled out of the naked land. Through his glasses John Lourdes scanned the desolate streets, "It seems to be deserted."

Soon after, out of the stark silence a voice came echoing up the long rift of that slim valley. Growing louder, they came to realize it was a woman's voice. Hain called out, "Efendi . . . upon the rock."

She was there. Hundreds of feet up that straight stone rockface and how in god's name had she gotten there? She wore a burka which from such a distance looked black. The wind blew wildly the garment and the veil and she seemed oblivious to all.

As they rode past the abandoned dwellings they watched the woman high up on that ledge clasp a hand to her breast in a manner of beseechment. She called to the heavens and then she threw her arms out wide. None understood her words, for they were not words at all but rather some mad undressed cry.

There came a rolling wave of thunder and wires of lightning and John Lourdes saw a flash of silver in the dust by a doorway. He turned the Arabian and walked it to the spot and leaned from the saddle. The others had drawn their mounts around and he trotted up alongside the priest to hand him the bracelet he found there.

The storm came sweeping out of the east where they rode four abreast their heads bowed against the rain. They pressed on into the night for a shelter the guide knew of. They rode the ridgeline where the rain poured down through faults and crevasses and seams in the slope to the plain below, and in a momentary flash of lightning what they saw there was gone before they were sure.

They called to each other and pointed and asked if what each saw, they saw, and they rode on vigilantly watching, and there came in time another drum of thunder and the crack of lightning and what they had seen, was in fact what was there.

A city of tents in orderly rows through the trampled brush and mud for what seemed miles. Lines of caissons dripping rain, lines of mounts picketed, blocks of supply wagons and medical wagons and ammunition wagons, all dripping rain.

The Turkish army there, then gone in darkness. The priest turned toward Hain and began to berate him. The dragoman joined in. The one word John Lourdes heard repeated was—*nazar*. And even when the guide whipped his mount and rode off, they yelled at his back, "*Nazar.*"

Under a vast ledge stood an abandoned shelter of stone and mud. A dilapidated shell, but still large enough for men and mounts. There was a firepit for warmth, and the air was smoky and damp, and John Lourdes had the dragoman translate the last of the letters and dispatches. To that end John Lourdes was not only searching for anything that might directly affect their survival, but be an indictment of what he had seen so far in the country.

The guide sat alone in a miserable state. He had taken to drinking the wine and sitting crosslegged before the fire. Beset by self-pity he called John Lourdes to his side.

"They didn't curse me for the shelter?" he whispered.

"What the hell are you talking about?"

Hain ran his fingers across his eyes, "*Nazar* . . . it was not my fault coming upon the army."

"Back on the ridge," said John Lourdes. "I heard that word. What does it mean?"

"The evil eye, efendi. They say is on me."

It took John Lourdes a moment to understand. "I see."

"I lost my *boncuk* during the escape from Erzurum."

"And what in God's name is a—"

"*Boncuk* . . . *boncuk*. Something you wear. On your being. A . . . amulet. It protects against evil spirits." He glanced at the priest and the dragoman. He told John Lourdes, "I will get one in Van. I swear it. There is no evil eye on me."

John Lourdes did not know what to say except, "Keep drinking."

He went to leave, but Hain would not let go of his arm. "This was a fine place once. I have lived many lives, efendi. Some bad, some not so bad. This was one of the lives."

He would have gone on but for the dragoman calling to John Lourdes. Something had been discovered in one of the letters. It was from a member of the Special Organization to a friend in Van.

"Do you know of the Ten Commandments?" said the old one.

"I know the ones I was taught by my mother and the priests. Thou shalt not kill. Thou shalt not—"

"No," said the dragoman, gravely. "These Ten Commandments were created by two doctors . . . Nazim and Shakir. They of the Special Organization. People know these commandments exist, but none have ever seen an official document. And the government denies they exist at all. But this letter, though not official—"

The dragoman explained to the priest about the contents of the letter. The priest took the letter. He read aloud in that burned voice and the dragoman translated, ". . . Destroy all Armenian societies . . . Collect arms . . . Provoke massacres . . . Send them to provinces such as Baghdad and Mosul and wipe them out on the road, or when they get there . . . Apply all measures to exterminate every man under fifty . . . carry away the families of all who succeed in escaping and apply measures to cut them off from all connection with their native place . . . All actions begin everywhere simultaneously, and thus leave no time for preparation of defensive measures . . . Pay attention to the strictly confidential nature of these instructions, which may not go beyond two or three parties . . ."

When the priest was finished reading he stared at the letter. He folded it back the way it was. He handed it not to the dragoman but to John Lourdes. As he did he repeated part of what he'd read. The dragoman again translated, "Pay attention . . . to . . . the confidential nature of these instructions . . . and do not allow it to go on beyond two or three parties."

John Lourdes took out his notebook and handing it to the dragoman said, "Would you please translate that letter for me line by line, so I can add it to my report and pass on the information"

John Lourdes rose and went through that crumbling doorway and stood looking into a rain that fell from the ledge roof in long full streams. He lit a cigarette and just let the night come in. There was something about these men that had the feel of childhood and memories. As if they were part of the barrio and railroad yard of his youth along the Rio Grande where he had been witness to stories told around the fires of poverty and class and color.

He looked back into the shelter. The priest had come about and was watching him. No, not watching, but rather, studying him. Constructing the human through brief impressions and taking measure.

fourteen

HEN THEY VENTURED forth, they rode toward the eye of the sun, ever vigilant to the horizon and threat of military patrols. They hid in a deep ravine as a column of Turkish cavalry made a sweep of the plain before them. They followed their trail of battered grass to its terminus, then pushed south further into the reaches of a land marked by knotted mounds of stone and long straights of grass. Nearly invisible they were against the vast undertaking that was the earth before them.

In the course of their journey they came upon small groups of refugees who would scatter and run from their approach, not knowing who or what the riders may be. Most were orphaned children and they would disappear into the trailless hills or forested slopes, and no amount of calling to them, no offer of food or friendship, allayed their fears or caused them to return.

At a creek they rode upon a small cluster of Armenians. A raggletag troop of families that looked to have been beaten and nearly starved. They did not have time to flee, for the horsemen had come too suddenly from a grotto of trees, and many just threw themselves prostrate to the earth and pleaded for their lives.

Even as Malek and the dragoman patiently explained, even as they offered food, the poor and beaten souls only wanted them away, for they represented danger. To John Lourdes this was a telling and pitiful testament to an ultimate state of defeat.

Among their number was an old priest. He wore now the meager robes of a vagabond. He came forward and spoke to Malek. He knew of him, but he no longer considered Malek a priest. His tone was harsh, his judgment critical, "Examine thy soul," he said. "The inner eye demands self-consciousness."

Malek listened then bowed, and he said with his eyes downcast, "Father . . . self-consciousness leads as much to tragedy as it does to truth, for it can breed in modern man . . . inaction."

One afternoon they came upon a Roman aqueduct. The remains of this remarkable structure stretched eerily across the frontier before them. As they approached the horseman could see hanging by their feet from one of the high arches the naked bodies of three men long since dead.

"Kurds, did this," said the guide.

John Lourdes took out the Enfield and rested it across his saddle. They proceeded beneath that vast construct. Birds flew from their stony perches before the riders, birds with white wings and black crowns.

There was no trail where they rode now and when they came to a rise, they halted. Before them lay flat miles of grass that would easily drape their saddles. A wide, softly moving river cut a line right through the heart of it to the horizon. There were estuaries along the main channel and breaks where streams ribboned off invisibly.

John Lourdes took the field glasses from his pack and surveyed the country. It was quiet and still and the grass moved slow as an hour hand. The priest and the dragoman talked among themselves, and the dragoman asked, "Are we going?"

"I'm deciding."

John Lourdes focused on the line of the river. Studying the shores on both sides. There were horse tracks on the near one that marched out a few hundred yards to where the river made a soft curve. He took the glasses from his eyes. His face grew taut. "How good are you at tracks?" he said to the guide.

"I'm still alive, efendi."

"That about answers it."

He handed him the field glasses and explained, "The river . . . The shoreline this side . . . Tracks . . . See them?"

Hain looked, "I do."

"See where the river curves."

"Yes."

"The tracks just end there, don't they?"

"Yes, efendi. They just end there."

"Do you see tracks on the far shore where they might have crossed?"

"No."

"Do you see grass trampled where they rode inland?"

"No."

The guide took the glasses and handed them back to John Lourdes. "They could have ridden into the shallows and downstream that way."

"Maybe. But I don't think so. How many riders you say from those tracks?"

"A handful."

"Kurds?"

"Kurds."

"Bandits?"

"Worse."

"You know what I think?"

Hain rubbed at his lower lip, then he began to tap at it while he thought, "You think they are out there."

"I think something is out there."

While they conferred, the priest spoke with the dragoman, then started down the rise at a walk. The guide saw and told John Lourdes who swung his mount and cut the priest off before he got a dozen yards.

"What in the hell are you doing?"

The meaning was clear, and the priest answered, "Van." He jabbed an arm in the direction where he meant go. "Van," he said again.

John Lourdes shook his head. "No! Tell him there's something out there."

The dragoman said, "He means to go. No matter what's—"

"God damn him."

Malek tried to force his horse past John Lourdes.

"I'm here to get you to Van. And I'm telling you—"

"Van," ordered the priest.

John Lourdes reined in his mount. He made a sweeping gesture with an arm, "The path is yours . . . you obstinate bastard."

Malek pressed forward, and as he passed, John Lourdes grabbed the priest's gunbelt. He got a hand through and around it, jerking hard. The two horses sided each other, the riders momentarily locked together and struggling, the horses near stumbled.

The dragoman, exhausted as he was with age and the pain of

that broken wrist, pleaded with the priest to heed John Lourdes. But Malek would have none of it. He was determined to go on at any cost and kept pointing as he repeated, "Van . . . Van."

A gunshot cut the argument short.

It was the guide. He had fired his revolver, which now hung down at his side, smoke drifted up from the barrel. He grinned like someone who had succeeded at his purpose

The priest had been startled. The dispute silenced. John Lourdes now turned his attention to the matter at hand. He told Hain, "Get your rifle. Follow me. But keep back enough to lay down cover."

John Lourdes swung the Enfield up on his shoulder and started down the incline at a slow walk. From a pack on his saddle he took the flare gun and loaded it. He tucked extra flares into his vest pocket. They proceeded with caution. The long blades brushed against his saddle near soundlessly. The way before them was steeped in calm sunlight. John Lourdes was far out into that wild thicket when he brought the Arabian to a halt and ordered the guide to do the same.

He looked to the banks of the river where they'd seen the first tracks. He then sighted inland. In his mind he had been thinking— would it be possible for a rider to walk his mount slow enough, carefully brushing aside those long and willowy reeds so he might make a path that was near undiscoverable? And doing that, lay a snare.

He aimed the gun, but not skyward. He pulled the trigger. A hissing flare went like a runner just above the tips of all that long green silence. When it exploded stars of white fire burst and burnt and the air singed and small raw-hot tracers rained down into the tall savannah leaving tails of smoke. John Lourdes quickly followed with a second volley that topped the first in a wonder of reddish glare that made that small patch of the world look to be on fire.

Then, as if by alchemy, a horse came lurching up out of the reeds, its great head arching and snapping as it tried to shake off the hot spurs. A Kurd forked over the saddle and urged his mount toward them at a gallop. From that ocean of grass another half dozen bandits struck up into the sunlight baring muskets and scimitars and charged toward the riders.

By the time John Lourdes shouldered his Enfield the guide had wounded the first Kurd who now spun his horse about. The priest instructed the dragoman to take up a position and protect the pack animals. Then pulling his revolver from its holster, he started down the slope at a full run.

The fight took place at long range. The Kurds were badly outgunned. John Lourdes shot the horse from under one bandit trying to cross the river and outflank them. The short white pony he had been riding collapsed in the shoals and spilled the bandit, who came up soaking. He tried to make a run for the safety of the breaks but was hit, then hit again. He dropped down in the mud in a sitting position, his head tilted forward as if resting and there he died.

There were pockets of smoke everywhere. Two of the Kurds fled toward the far hills. Another, whose mount had been crippled, tried to escape on foot. One of the bandits was bearing down on John Lourdes, who had turned the Arabian toward the river to parry any threat the riders fleeing there might still present. The priest kicked his mount in pursuit to intercept the Kurd, who now shouldered a scimitar.

The guide yelled to John Lourdes, who leaned around. The priest had emptied his revolver, yet the Kurd came on. He was an enormous man with flowing hair, crouched over the long neck of his warhorse.

The priest was now between both men, trampling down the

grass full out. Before John Lourdes could take aim and fire, the two horseman met head on. The Kurd slashed with his blade, the priest did not try to avoid it. Rather, he drove his horse straight into the full force of the enemy.

The two beasts crushed against each other. In their cries, the wrack of agony. The horse the Kurd rode toppled back over on itself, the one the priest sat atop dropped like a stone. The blood grunts of the two men could be heard tearing at each other and there was nothing but vast green waves and the sky until a scimitar rose up and the steel shined for an instant before it scythed down with a hellish whoosh. Then all was still.

The dragoman called to the priest, the priest did not answer. Behind the advance of a blade a path appeared. It was Malek. He hobbled past John Lourdes to the river. The naked hardness of his stare revealed nothing.

John Lourdes followed him. The priest stood on the shore and threw the scimitar into the water. Blood steamed from the blade as it sank. He kneeled and washed his hands. John Lourdes climbed out of the saddle and stood not far from him.

The priest looked at the water dripping from his hands. "I am a failure. As a priest." he said. "At the calling I was born for. If only we could pick and choose what god was watching. What men we would be. What heavens would open for us. Maybe we require lost paradises as an excuse."

Malek grew quiet. He looked up at the young foreigner. "You were right before." He pointed to one of the dead.

"You know," said John Lourdes, "I've got about ten thousand questions I'd like to ask you."

The priest scooped up more water and washed his face. Beads dripped from his matted beard.

Hain and the dragoman canted up through the reeds. The guide told John Lourdes, "The priest's horse is dead. But one of the Kurds has been gracious enough to will him a mount."

The priest and the dragoman began to talk amongst themselves. The old one turned to John Lourdes. "Malek says you think quick and well. And you are crafty. He wonders. How did you come by this? Are you trained for the military?"

John Lourdes considered the question. "The truth is, I try to think like my father."

The dragoman explained to the priest who asked, "Your father then, what was he?"

John Lourdes pulled himself up into the saddle. He sat there looking out over the river then answered without shame or guilt. "He was a criminal . . . and a common assassin."

PART II

Van

fifteen

FREEDOM DEMANDS RESISTANCE.

Van was to be the flashpoint of that resistance. It was there the first true fight of what the future was to look like would be waged by the Armenian people.

Even as the military and civil authorities of Van went about their draconian measures against the Armenian community, the resistance clandestinely exercised its determination of will. Foot soldiers and artillery would be confronted by well-planned and cunning countermeasures.

In the Armenian quarter youths lounged at street corners watching silently for the gendarmes. When spotted they passed the word to women who stood sentry at windows and on rooftops beside alleys where members of the Dashnaktsutyun—the Freedom Party—prepared the tactics of battle. At night, old men sat in lamplit doorways smoking their *chibouks* and playing with the little ones as they kept guard for those who carried buckets of dirt from a honeycomb of tunnels that ran for blocks connecting homes and warehouses to be used as—*teerks*—manned fighting stations.

The morning after Alev Temple returned from Constantinople, she commandeered a wagon from the American Hospital to carry home a patient recovering from surgery. She was to drive him out to the suburb of Aikesden, which was part of the Armenian quarter in Van known as the Gardens. It was a place of orchards and enclosures hidden beneath the reach of the willows grown up around them. In the courtyard where she arrived with the patient was a caravan of camels burdened with heavy wood casks of kerosene. One broke loose as they were unroped. Falling to the earth it cracked open. It was filled not with paraffin, but heavy black Mauser pistols wrapped in cloth. German weapons sold by Turkish smugglers to Armenian *fedayeen*. The guns were grabbed up by the women and children who hid them in their garments then ran away.

THAT NIGHT IN Van, Alev Temple dined at the home of Doctor Charles Ulster. He ran the hospital in the American compound, which also made him a representative of the American government.

At the table with Ulster and his wife, were Edwin Blake, attaché to the British Consulate and a man named Harmon Frost. Frost was a character all to himself. He looked much like the former president Theodore Roosevelt, a comparison that delighted him. His business card read Import and Export, but that meant almost anything in these times. He was a decidedly political creature, and it had been hinted that he was with the American State Department, running clandestine operations in alliance with the Entente.

There was gunfire in the streets that night. More than usual. There had been a steady escalation over the last few weeks so that each new nightfall brought with it a rising sense of terror.

Dinner conversation tended toward the political, or any immediate threat to survival. That night one subject dominated—the priest. Edwin Blake had been at the German Consulate when word arrived that a small handful of Armenian *fedayeen* had bombed their way into the prison at Erzurum and freed Malek. They had even managed his escape from the city.

The Turkish government in Van was on high alert, for it was understood Malek meant to make for Van. From the Citadel, which the Turkish government controlled, cavalry had been seen making their way into the frontier to intercept this band of anarchists.

News of the priest's escape had already reached the streets of Van. Even refugees streaming in from the outlying districts who had evaded the massacres knew the priest was free. It was as if a telepathic communication was carrying word that riders were coming to overthrow the order.

"On my way here," said Edwin Blake, "I heard some refugees talking. They said the Cyclops had fallen."

The doctor's wife did not understand.

"That's what they call the prison at Erzurum," said Alev. "The Cyclops."

The name was born from the lone guard tower, with its great wheel of gas lanterns always turning that could be seen in all quarters of the city and far into the darkness of the plain. This everburning eye had become a symbol of repression and torture.

"The Cyclops," repeated Edwin Blake. "They have rural imaginations, don't they. Folkloric, anyway."

"At least they're up on their mythology," said Frost. He took a drink of beer that he had shipped in from the States especially.

"They're a superstitious lot. With their *nazar* and all the other nonsense."

"Don't forget their religion," said Alev, "which I believe is the same as yours."

"And yours," said Frost.

"Yes . . . and I have respect for both."

"I'm sure there is an adage for the moment, but the outcome to such a conversation does not interest me."

There was an increase of gunfire and Alev excused herself and stood and went to the veranda where she could look out over the city.

Van was built in two sections. There was the fortress with its walled city that towered over Lake Van, and there were the Gardens. Between the two stood the Turkish quarters. The American compound was in the Gardens, just blocks from Turkish homes and shops. It was on a slight rise so it commanded a view and could, in turn, be seen from quite a distance.

The night was unusually warm. There was much activity in the streets. Armenian music was being played on Victorolas throughout their quarter as an act of defiance. Alev looked toward the walled city and the fortress, with its dusty battlements and cuneiform inscriptions from when this land belonged to the children of Noah. There was an assembly of torchlights at the gate, which usually meant troops were on the move.

Alev's thoughts were with Malek. When he was just out of the novitiate he had worked beside her parents in the hostels and infirmaries. He had baptized her, he had been priest at her first communion and confirmation. He had been family friend and confidant. And his face was the face of holidays and holy days, and it fell to him to perform the mass at the funeral for the murdered Temples.

Mrs. Ulster joined her.

"To some," Alev said, "This is all just political chess."

"Ahh," said her hostess. "Why is it that the most far-reaching proclamations come from the most shortsighted people?"

Alev looked at this nurse, with her wispy hair and glasses behind which were eyes touched with just a tint of resignation.

"Why?"

"Because those people can't see far enough to even know they are shortsighted."

From the porch the doctor called urgently to the women. They joined him and the other men on the far side of the wood-frame house. Between the Armenian quarter and the Turkish quarter defensive positions had been clearly established. Trenches dug, shooting holes bored into mud walls, makeshift breastworks across streets and open fields. A fire had begun at the southern end of that perimeter in the neighborhood of Arak. A block of Armenian homes and shops were being consumed by flames that rose on the wind and yawed violently against a black sky. The wind drove embers across rooftops and down streets and they looked from the compound like an army of forged locust on the move. Units from the Fireman's College rushed past in wagons and *arabas* and whatever else they could conscript to reach the fire before the neighborhood was turned to ash.

The doctor pointed to Toprak-Kala Hill. From the Turkish barracks there came the flash of rifle fire, then the sharp crack of the shots. The Armenian barricades that fronted it returned fire. The shooting intensified. The dim voices of the men shouting in confusion or giving orders could be heard through the fraying wind.

From the Citadel hill near the military school, there came the thunder of artillery and the shrill flight of shells. A building beyond the breastworks was lifted in a quake of dust and brick, then crumbled down upon itself. In the smoking crater of its rubble appeared a thin wick of fire.

"Why all this tonight? Why?" said the doctor's wife.

"Retribution," said Frost.

"For what?" said Alev.

"Because the Armenian favors death over his own government," said Frost. "Because the Armenian is for the Entente. Because the Armenian won't die quickly or gracefully. Because the Turk can't kill him, even when they outnumber him. Miss Temple . . . is that the kind of answer most suited to your sensibilities?"

"There is, though, a reason for tonight," said Edwin Blake. He turned to Frost, so he might finish.

"Yes, there is a reason," said Frost. "Miss Temple . . . earlier this evening it seems some daring citizen from the Gardens went to the Police and Telegraph Station of Khatch Pogotz and painted on the wall there—*Malek is coming.*"

ALEV TEMPLE HAD been told by two women working for the Danish Red Cross to look for tall, strangely made crucifixes standing about three kilometers south of Van and visible from the road to Bashkale. The women had come up the Tigris from Mosul. They had worked the desert camps with their displaced and starving Armenians, but nothing in their training or experience had prepared them for what they saw on the Bashkale Road.

Alev had gone to the site of the fire the following morning. Smoke from the rubble greyed an otherwise sunny and clear street. Humanitarian workers were on the scene helping the homeless and the shopkeepers deal with the tragedy. This is where Alev met the women with the Danish Red Cross.

Carson Ammons, a newspaperman with the *New York Herald,* was also there taking pictures. He recognized Miss Temple from that night in Constantinople at the Pera Palas Hotel and her speech on the front steps. She told him about her conversation with the horrified Danish women to convince him there might be something to photograph south of the city.

The crucifixes stood upright against the clean blue light of day. The face of the landscape was rock strewn with broken swales of thicket. Tall, slender crosses marked the silence with their long shadows. The bodies were in a shallow decline. They were infested with flies and creatures that scurried through the weeds at their approach. Even the wolves had had their hour of feeding. But it was the crucifixes, with their sharpened and bloody tips, that stood out in the shimmery light before them.

"No one in the world would print a photograph of this," said the newspaperman.

Alev sat upon a rock. She made herself look at the bodies of the young girls, with legs spread where the crosses had speared them. "Someone will," she said.

ALEV TEMPLE SPENT the night at the German missionary orphanage with the director Herr Sporri, writing letters to ambassadors and influential Turkish men of good will who stood against these ongoing and ever-worsening atrocities, describing for them the devolving situation in Van and what she herself had witnessed that day along the road to Bashkale.

She lay that night in the hallway of the orphanage but sleep did not come. The road and the crosses held fast in her mind and moved from place to place inside her like a ghostly poison. The din of gunfire was nothing as it dawned on her for the first time she was truly an orphan. A child of this tragedy as much as the children who called the mission their home.

She was weary and frightened, and she cried into the covers so no one would hear. She prayed, but she did not ask God for strength or will, but rather he keep her human so that she might embrace every hurt for the promise of beauty and goodness.

Alev woke to the sound of screaming.

It was not until a bedlam of children rushed past and crowded up into the windows to look out that she understood it was not her who had been screaming.

In the cool hours before dawn a group of young Armenian women had started off from an outlying district for the marketplace. To be careful, they flocked together for protection. But, as long sleek traces of light made their way up through the dusty thoroughfares, the young women were approached by two Turkish soldiers. In the confrontation that followed one of the girls was dragged off to be violated. The others took to pleading in the street, calling out in desperation toward the sleepy buildings for someone, anyone, to come to their friend's aid.

This encounter had taken place within sight of the orphanage, and by the time Alev Temple and Herr Sporri were running toward the scene, two young Armenian men had angrily approached the soldiers.

The young men demanded answers. What began as a verbal altercation escalated quickly. The Armenians were adamant with their recriminations for what the soldiers had done. Alev Temple tried to use her credentials to keep the conflict from descending into immediate violence until higher authorities could take control of the moment and see that justice prevailed.

The murder of the two young men was executed by the soldiers there in the street with swift efficiency. There followed moments of mortal silence and fear. Alev stared in anguish as she leaned over one of the dead. Blood on his white shirt, on his black coat. He wore an amulet on his collar. Everything about her parents' murder flooded up in ways that were unimaginable. She looked up at the soldiers. They were cool and brazen and beyond her reach. A wave of rage went through her. She wanted to see them dead. Dead there in the gutter and spit upon, and she understood how a sea of violence begins with a drop of hate.

Alev Temple helped load the bodies into a cart. And all that day she could not help but think . . . Such a tragic and pointless incident . . . It was not militarily important, it was not historically significant or manifestly strategic. But, it perfectly symbolized the nature of the antagonists' conflict. It was the ageless story of violation and epithet, recrimination and gunshot. And so, on the morning of April 20, 1915, shortly after dawn, in the city of Van, the war there had been served up on a street corner.

sixteen

O N THE EVENING of the twentieth, four riders ascended the hills above Lake Van. Dark silhouettes against the even darker escarpment they climbed. For the last two days they had circumvented villages being put to the sword, and peasants under guard being herded along dusty roads to their demise. There were endless patrols and mercenaries, and even upon reaching that gunblack and silent crest they could not be sure for their safety.

The men dismounted. Van was a small island of light in the distance. They could hear the faint concussion of artillery carrying across the waters below. Pockets of fire in one quadrant of the city seemed to be burning out of control.

The dragoman told John Lourdes, "The fires are coming from the Armenian quarter."

John Lourdes got the field glasses from his pack and went to the edge of the bluff. There were orderly fires along the lakeshore and stations of torchlight on what he suspected were the roads in and out of Van. He handed the field glasses to the dragoman.

"If we're going in, we should try it tonight."

The old one handed the field glasses to Malek. The two men spoke briefly. The dragoman told John Lourdes, "We go tomorrow?"

"Tomorrow?"

"That is his wish."

John Lourdes glanced at the priest who was now scrupulously looking over the valley floor. "Does he know what comes with tomorrow?"

"How do you mean?"

"Daylight."

"Ah. I understand."

"We've beat the hell out of these mounts getting here. Look at them. Van is about eight, ten kilometers. We could buy most of that ground in the dark. Maybe . . . If we're lucky . . . all of it. But in daylight—"

"Tomorrow," said the dragoman as he went and exhausted sat.

The priest had seen enough. He handed the glasses to John Lourdes.

The priest walked up to Hain. He had been squatting by the horses and thumbing tobacco into his *chibouk*. He quickly stood when the priest was before him.

"Can you cut me a staff?"

The guide, unsure, said, "A walking staff?"

"A staff. As tall as I am and then half again."

"That high . . . Yes."

"And when you shave it, it must be as wide as a lira. But no wider."

"As wide as a lira?"

"But no wider."

"I understand." He paused, "What is it for?"

"Can you make the staff?"

"I can."

"Will you make the staff?"

"I will."

"Make the staff, and you will find out what it is for."

Each man took a short watch while the others slept. Cannon fire ceased after midnight, but for the occasional shell lobbed into the quarter to keep the Armenians under the constant strain of threat. If what John Lourdes saw from the bluffs did not mean what it did, the lights and the fires in that unrecorded void would stand as a beautiful sight. Easily majestic and mysterious. Like the country itself. The priest came and sat quietly beside John Lourdes. He washed his wounded and painful feet.

"You will be shown appreciation in Van." Knowing he was not understood the priest pointed to the city, "And due respect."

"We should have tried to get in tonight."

The two men turned their attention to the frontier.

The dragoman awoke. The priest began talking and motioned to John Lourdes. The dragoman listened and translated, "Malek wants you to know . . . this was the country of the Uratu. And the cradle of Armenia. In the lake is an island . . . Akdamar. The remains of a great church are there. It is all that is left of a palace and orchards and parks built by the Prince Gagik. They say the palace had golden cupolas and the Prince was sent from Samara a gold crown with gems and pearls . . . and a robe and belt and sword also of gold that glittered so it made the lake appear on fire." Malek paused and grew reflective and what he said finally, the dragoman told John Lourdes. "Malek knows these are just stories, but he said to me wishfully, 'Ah . . . what tales, my son.'"

Malek looked now at John Lourdes' face and he reached toward that face and John Lourdes' head angled slightly, and the priest rubbed the skin along the cheek with his thumb. He then did the same to the skin along his own cheek.

DAWN CAME UPON them. A fan of light creeping over the mountains. The windswept crags of Akdamar Island and the ruins of the domed church there took on a golden hue. The guide walked past John Lourdes and pointed the staff he had finally finished preparing toward the snowy peak of a mountain at the eastern rim of the world.

"Ararat," he said. "The ark of history resides there." He spat. "Noah should have taken more women and fewer sons."

He went over to the priest and the old one, who were sitting against the rockface and planning privately.

"It is done," he said, holding out the staff.

"I see," said Malek. "And I see the branch you chose is straighter than your conscience."

The priest took the staff. As he ran his hand along the smooth shaft the dragoman removed from his shirt a small bundle. He handed it to the priest as John Lourdes walked up and stood with the guide.

The bundle was of fine red cloth and the dragoman bowed and kissed it. Malek set the staff aside as the packet was placed in his hands. The priest too lifted the bundle and he kissed it and then he stood. In each hand he took an edge and then carefully he let the cloth fall loose.

It was a flag of three vertical stripes seamed together. One red, one green, one blue. "This is one of the flags created by the good Father Alishan," said the dragoman. He looked toward Mount

Ararat and told John Lourdes, "The colors are of the rainbow over the ark when the flood had ended."

The dragoman had been carrying rope, as well, for this moment. He handed it to Malek who began slipping the heavy twine through knotted loops along the flag's edge and lashing them to the staff.

The priest went about this task in a precise and ceremonial manner and John Lourdes could not help but remember the factory in the barrio where his mother worked as an immigrant from Mexico sewing American flags. With its tarred roof and stifling air filled with specks of cloth from the cutters' work. And the ear-numbing endless drone of the machines the women sat crouched over in that windowless brick shell, sweating so badly their skin was like drenched brown earth.

And there was that first summer his mother had taken him downtown to San Jacinto Park for the Fourth of July celebration. Flags hung everywhere. From lampposts and office buildings and rooftops and children waving them and women, and a dog wore one as a bandana and it shot past him at a full-out run. They even were draped over the legs of broken men confined to wheelchairs who had served their country well, only to be forgotten except on such days of remembrance.

"Look," his mother had told him. "We helped make all of this."

The way she had said, "We helped make all of this." Her words had such authenticity of soul and legitimate pride. She had crossed a pumice wasteland on foot to reach that moment, and it was exactly what he saw on the faces of the priest and the dragoman.

Then, inexplicably, John Lourdes' father came to him in the last moments of his life. On that sidewalk with his back to a church wall dying in the Mexican sun and holding up John Lourdes' notebook with the last few words he had written to amend his failure of a life: "Son—forgive me."

"Efendi."

The thought had came upon John Lourdes with the same overwhelming surprise that was exactly his father.

"Efendi."

The page from his notebook—that page—had been in his wallet ever since. "What," he said to the guide.

The guide was looking at the flag. "The priest is not the journey, is he?"

"No," said John Lourdes. "He is not the journey."

⁓

THEY STRIPPED THE mounts down to bare essentials. They cut the pack horses loose. Anything they did not need to carry was cast aside. With field glasses John Lourdes and the dragoman went about surveying the flats for their run to Van.

There was sporadic gunfire in the city. The occasional volley shells of artillery. There were soldiers along the lake, and others taking sailboats up the further shore. It was the guard stations along the road that had to be considered. And a canal known as the Shamiram that needed to be crossed.

There was one isolated wooden bridge with just three guards who seemed intent on firing at something poking up out of the ground. It was too distant to tell what it might be, but puffs of dirt constantly pricked up from the earth around it.

"They're not very good shots," said the dragoman.

"Let's hope we're seeing them at their best."

John Lourdes, unlike the dragoman, thought he knew what they were shooting at, but said nothing.

The priest had climbed into the saddle and was reaching for the flag staff, which he had spiked into the ground when the guide approached. He was holding what appeared to be a chalice of burnished gold. He offered it to the priest.

"And what is this?"

"It's a chalice," said the guide.

"That is not what I meant."

"I thought you might like to have it."

Malek studied it carefully. "Was this also willed to you?"

"It was willed. Yes."

"You seem to be one of those souls who is constantly being willed things."

"In all fairness. Your company seems to assure it."

"I see," said the priest.

"It's not a bad chalice. As far as chalices go."

"As far as they go. What would you have me do with it?"

Hain shrugged. "Whatever priests do with chalices."

This small company started down the crest keeping to a breaker of trees. Once on the plain they maneuvered the landscape descending into long swales for cover, only to rise again into the bleached sunlight.

There was still breakfast smoke from the camps along the shore. To the south, cavalry headed to Van at a slow walk. The riders crossed through a broad swath of trampled grass where the march of foot soldiers led toward Persia and then, breaching a stand of willows, descended into a river where women washed clothes upon the rocks. When they saw these haggard men and their weapons and that flag whose colors rippled along the water's surface they rose up screaming and ran.

Out of the trees the women scattered like a flock of wild birds. The riders reorganized in the shallows, and John Lourdes separated from them, coming up out of the trace straight for the guard station at the plank bridge that crossed the canal.

He saw the women come to a road where there was a cart laden with barrels and crates, followed by men making their way from Van. The women shrieked and they pointed and the men gathered around them. They listened and they looked and then one took off running for the same guard station John Lourdes approached. He was shouting but too far off to be heard.

John Lourdes drew near the bridge. The guards were still shooting at the target, but they stopped when they saw a rider trotting toward them. They raised their arms to halt and as John Lourdes got close enough he could see they had been passing the time firing at the desiccated head of a man.

John Lourdes played the innocent traveler from Mexico, offering papers written in Turkish for them to inspect. Each took a turn going line by line and they eyed him and they eyed the horse and the weapons in his scabbard. He couldn't understand a word they were saying, but it wouldn't surprise him if they were sizing up his head to play bookend to the one there in the brush.

Their strange chatter began to subside, and the one with John Lourdes' papers had even gone so far as to stretch out an arm to return them, when the man sprinting toward the guards could finally be heard.

The soldiers were trying to make sense of what was being shouted when one of their number spotted three riders dash from the trees bunched up along the river. Their mounts were kicking up great clots of earth and the flag rippled and snapped and what the soldiers saw they could not quite believe.

John Lourdes booted his horse forward and with one sweep grabbed his papers. By the time the soldier's head turned John Lourdes' other arm rose with his automatic aimed and ready. The soldier stood there rigid without understanding.

The impact at that range shot blood out his back about a dozen meters. The Arabian jolted and the soldiers drew their weapons and scattered toward John Lourdes' flanks. His horse reared and backpedaled and John Lourdes' shots went wild.

The guide was leaning into the neck of his mount with a rifle. He fired and one of the soldiers was hit in the thigh and the bone went clear through the pant leg. He was left on the ground snaked up in agony while the other soldier made it to the edge of the canal beside the bridge. He fired from a prone position at John Lourdes who leaned against the Arabian's shoulder and ran him up onto the bridge and shot down through the slatted boarding.

When the soldier ran out of ammunition John Lourdes saw him take a metallic cylinder from his belt and strike its fuse against a rock. John Lourdes kicked the Arabian forward to clear the bridge as the soldier went to fling what was a grenade. A volley of shots from the riders approaching took him apart and the grenade rolled beneath the bridge supports and blew.

Planking pocked the water. Smoke curled and drifted and the concussion of the grenade reached well into the plain. The riders reined in at the water's edge. John Lourdes shouted for them to come on. Their mounts had to be maneuvered one at a time, and the remaining plankboard shuddered and creaked under their weight as they crossed.

Along the lakeshore and from Van, John Lourdes could see sunlight winking off field glasses. To the south the cavalry patrol had turned and were after them at a hard gallop and it was three kilometers to safety.

They were a slender arrow upon that ancient plain aimed for Van. Troops were on the move to intercept them. Riflefire dotted the sky but too far for an accounting.

They were like something imagined coming out of a long sleep to cross a road then push on through windtwisting grass where lay forgotten *khatchkars* like great boats of stone, their inscriptions steeped in history and salvation.

Along the rooftops of the Armenian quarter men pointed toward the flag and waved their hats, shouting the riders on. From the barricades armed citizens charged out on foot followed by a coterie on horseback that set a perimeter and lay down coverfire.

Everywhere there was shooting. Another discharge of artillery and the arcing rain of a shell landed before the riders and their mounts skittered and bolted sideways. The men separated and re-formed past a vapor of smoke and dust. John Lourdes could see the Armenians along the quarter rooftops and manning the barricades. For the most part they did not wear kaftans and loose-fitting trousers but rather European suitcoats and dark pants and square-cut vests. These were not trained soldiers but shopkeepers and cobblers, bankers and tradesmen, whose forebears and kinsmen were being carried home to them in the body of that flag. The priest and his vanguard of riders cleared the perimeter and ascending the earthen battlements in a torrent of hooves and dust leapt the trench and entered Van.

seventeen

A DELUGE OF PEOPLE crowded the horse-men. They helped the weary dragoman from his saddle as they would a cherished uncle. The men around the priest wept and the women touched the hem of his filthy robe as if it were a sacred vestment. The young begged for the flag and he passed it to their outstretched arms. They ran with it in a pack across the street. There it was lifted to a world of grasping hands that reached out from a balcony railing. It hung there momentarily in their arms before it rose up again to where a boy had been lowered from the ledge, his legs gripped tight by others. And when he had it firmly, they hoisted him up then there it was on the roof for all to see.

Those around John Lourdes patted at his legs and fought to shake his hand. He had no idea what they were saying and he repeatedly asked if anyone spoke English or Spanish.

"I speak English . . . a little."

He looked behind him. Standing atop the rubble of a destroyed building was Alev Temple.

"You," he said.

"Kismet," she said.

She came up beside his horse.

"You said that word once before. I don't know what it means."

"Kismet . . . Fate."

"Fate," he said.

"Do you remember at the boat, I asked—"

"If we should ever meet again . . . I remember, Alev."

She was pleased. She put a hand out and he leaned from the saddle, and they shook, and she held his hand a long time and put her other hand over his also.

The people began to talk to John Lourdes through Alev Temple, who now served as his official interpreter and biographer with unswerving admiration and sincerity.

"You made many friends today."

"I need something to balance the ledger," he said.

He glanced toward the direction from where they'd come, and she understood.

"I want you to look. Up the street. That hill." She pointed. "With the two-story hospital and wall. That's the American Mission compound. Doctor Ulster. Go there. I will see there's a place for you. I have to leave you now. For a friend."

She pointed to the priest and walked off.

⌒

THE DOCTOR OFFERED John Lourdes a small room in the mission residences that opened onto a covered porch. The room had a bed with a frame and a pillow. Against the far wall was a Shaker bureau with a mirror and porcelain bowl for washing. Through the open door he could see the hospital and school buildings and part of the church roof beyond.

Everything suddenly just breathed home. Even the still air was Texas. And yet, home felt far away, farther away than miles or distance. His heart said home was fleeing him, receding into the frontiers of memory. That the ropes and ties of his birth were coming undone, beyond his will or power.

"How the hell do I get away from here?"

John Lourdes looked up quickly. In the doorway stood a man with a gruff face and large teeth and a bushy moustache clipped at the upper lip.

"How do I get back to a god damn steak and good scotch and telephones and movie houses and women who dress like women but drink like men. Mr. Lourdes . . . I'm Harmon Frost." He pointed through the doorway. "May I?"

"Of course."

John Lourdes stood, and the men shook hands. Frost looked the room over, John Lourdes' belongings over.

"That was quite an entrance today. That's all the good citizens are talking about." Frost reached into his suitcoat pocket. "Cigarette?"

He took out a pack, kept one for himself then handed it to John Lourdes. "I have a steady supply coming in. That and good pilsner beer. Keep it."

He lit John Lourdes' cigarette and then his own. "Does that character on the porch belong to you?"

Frost meant the guide. Hain had taken a blanket and propped it up to make a tent.

"He was my guide from Trebizond."

"How's his English?"

"Good enough to pass bad checks anywhere in the States."

"We can't have that."

Frost closed the door.

"That was quite a feat getting the priest out of the Cyclops."

"Cyclops? What is that?"

"It's what the rurals here call the prison at Erzurum. The tower . . . the light . . . like a single eye. How was it coming down country?"

"I kept a running report in my notebook. What they call deportations are actually exterminations. I've seen dead on the Black Sea . . . outside Erzurum . . . to the north and west of here."

"Tell me about the priest."

John Lourdes went over to the window and looked out. "He's committed. He's rock hard tough. And smart. He knows what he wants, and he's on a course to get it."

"And what does he want?"

"You saw today."

"I was not there."

"The flag."

"He wants a country."

"Yes."

"Of course. I was wondering what he wants on a more practical level."

"I don't think the priest and the word 'practical' spend much time together."

"Well. Is he workable?"

"Workable?"

"Yes."

"Workable how?"

"Manageable."

John Lourdes flicked his cigarette ash out the window. "To what end?"

"I think you understand what I mean."

"I know what you mean. I just don't know what it means."

Harmon Frost ignored this. He started for the door. "Stay close to Malek for the next few days. Keep me appraised of his movements. I'll be convening a meeting with him soon. You'll be there."

"Sir?"

"Yes."

"Money promised to the guide."

"Ah . . . a practical man."

At the door Frost hesitated before heading out. "I want you to understand something. We are not here as liberators. This is about . . . The term I . . . *We* use . . . is resource control."

"Sir?"

"Resource control. Everything and anything that can be manufactured, shipped, mined, grown, merchandised, including order and good will."

—⁀

HE STOOD WATCHING Harmon Frost exit the compound. John Lourdes' superior at the Bureau of Investigation, Justice Knox, had a world view that he defined as "the practical application of strategy." A major tenant of this philosophy—man's central need and desire was for bureaucracy. Not freedom, not rebellion, not individuality. Man craved effective bureaucracy, the ultimate expression of which was order. And to accomplish this, dispassion to events, situations and people was mandatory.

Resource control—there was an energetic leanness to the phrase, and an intellectual ingenuity fraught with interpretation. It seemed to John Lourdes a determined extension, if not the inevitable evolvement of—the practical application of strategy.

He had wondered if the heart of the world was hardening over centuries. His friend and ally Wadsworth Burr answered, "The world has been the same since Scripture. The only thing that changes is our ability to describe what the world truly is. Peace teaches us nothing, tells us nothing. Peace is the nap between wakeful hours of war. That's where man presents his true nature."

John Lourdes stepped out of the doorway. At the far end of the porch sat the guide. By him were his tent and belongings. He drank tea and smoked, and seeing John Lourdes he raised his cup, "The people here kindly gave me tea, and they smiled. Then they told me I had lice."

John Lourdes leaned against a post supporting the roof, "You were listening, I bet."

The guide glanced at Harmon Frost, who was walking out the compound gate.

John Lourdes took from his vest pocket an envelope. He tossed it to Hain. The guide quickly went to work counting the lira. "Does he carry that much money on him all the time?"

"What are you gonna do with it?"

The guide raised his cup in a sort of toast, "I'm going to put it in the Bank of Hain."

John Lourdes understood and grinned. "Where, of course, you are the president."

His companion grandly waved a hand, "President . . . cashier . . . And I also wash the marble lavatory."

"We get you dry cleaned and into a nice suit . . . And goddamn . . . you're an American."

At the far end of the compound John Lourdes saw the priest

and a number of Armenian men follow Alev Temple into the sunlight between the dispensary and hospital.

"That relief worker and the priest are very close. Families very close. I heard."

John Lourdes squatted down next to the guide. He took a cigarette from the pack Frost had given him, then reached for Hain's pipe.

"I have a job for you."

He used the burning tobacco in the pipe to light his cigarette.

"There will be money."

"The job?"

John Lourdes' eyes went toward the hospital. "The priest."

"You have suspicions?"

"I have concerns."

"I am to be your eyes, then."

"When I cannot be."

"I understand, efendi." He then pointed.

Alev Temple was walking back up from the hospital alone. John Lourdes stood and walked down from the porch to meet her.

"Malek wanted to see the wounded . . . and the children."

"I'm sorry," said John Lourdes.

"Why?"

"For not being honest with you at the boat."

She put a hand on his arm as a way of saying it was all right. "By the way, you are invited to dinner at Doctor Ulster's."

"Are you to be there?"

"I invited you."

She then took John Lourdes by the arm and walked him off to where she felt confident they would not to be overheard.

"After dinner . . . men will come. Friends of the priest. They will want you to go with them."

"You are asking me, for them."

"Yes."

"And do you know why?"

"I was not entrusted with that."

eighteen

ITH DARKNESS, AGAIN came the artillery bombardment. The lightning from their barrels marked the night. A grove they shelled was burning out of control, row upon row of branches crackling into extinction. John Lourdes studied the exchanges as he shaved. Most of the shooting came from the Turkish quarter, the Armenian offering only occasional and controlled counterfire.

Before entering Ulster's cottage, he undid his shoulder holster and hung it over a bench on the porch. His shirt was wrinkled but clean, his hair combed. As grace was said, he stared at the table, at the plates and silverware and napkins neatly folded. When the doctor had put an amen to the prayer, his wife said, "Are you all right, John?"

What he truly felt he did not express. "I haven't sat at a table with plates and forks and—"

He stopped and just sat there.

"May I?" said Alev to their host.

Dr. Ulster nodded.

She rose and went to a makeshift breakfront and from a cabinet took a bottle of whiskey and poured a glass. This she set before John Lourdes.

"Thank you," he said.

After dinner, Alev Temple joined John Lourdes, who sat on the porch as he awaited the arrival of the men who would come for him. He smoked, and sipped the whiskey left in his glass. An occasional volley of gunfire overtook the stillness. They sat at the edge of the light from a lamp inside a window. Their shadows fell about their feet only to slip away into the dark. It was she who spoke first.

"I had this dream. I've had it a few times. I catch a firefly. You know . . . fireflies. I have it cupped in my hand and I peek at it through a little space I create between my two thumbs. Its tail flashes on and off. It is like a tiny heart beating in this cave of my making."

He listened. He went to sip from his drink, but did not. "Coming down country," he said, "was very bad. Very bad."

They were quiet again. She watched him smoke, he found comfort in the watching. In her eyes the lamplight caught like the firefly she dreamt of in her hands. She again was the first to speak.

"They say nothing is promised, but it would be wonderful if it were."

"My mother used to say 'the deeper the burden, the higher the beauty.'"

"I was sleeping at the German Mission orphanage the other night. And lying in bed I thought of my parents. And how I was now an orphan."

"I thought of home today."

"You mean that large state near California? Texas is near California?"

He looked into her unmarked smile. She had made him laugh. And she laughed also. As he drank the whiskey, she pulled her legs up and wrapped her arms around them. There they sat in the finely cast shadows until John Lourdes spoke, "I need to solicit your help."

He took from his shirt the pocket notebook. He opened it to a page where he had the letter tucked away.

"We took this from a Turkish soldier on route to Van. I had it translated. And there are notes I kept of all that happened or we saw. I would like you to make copies of it. Keep at least one. If anything should befall me, send my notebook to this gentleman." He had written Wadsworth Burr's name and address on a page he included in the envelope with the letter.

"Would you do that?"

"You knew you were giving me this before you came to dinner."

He did not get a chance to answer. "They're here," he said.

She looked across the compound. Three men in black coats stood near the gate lamps. John Lourdes rose and finished his whiskey. He walked over to the bench and took up his holster. He slipped on the shoulder strap and belted it.

As they walked to the gate, she said, "I'll make the copies, John."

"Yes," he said, "I had planned to give you the notebook."

The men kept to the shadow side of the gate and spoke to Alev Temple in Armenian. Two carried rifles. The young man who happened to be in charge, a Mr. Zadian, did not. He had a bony, hard face, and he was already bald.

"I am the one who organized with Mr. Baptiste in Constantinople to get the priest here," said Mr. Zadian. "Will you come?"

The streets were a warren of shadows and incoming shells and riflefire and Mr. Zadian kept close to the building walls for protection. They proceeded down a narrow causeway of alleys making themselves as much of the dark as possible. They were a few dozen yards from the barricades and John Lourdes could make out that most of the gunfire was from the military barracks on Toprak-Kala Hill.

The passage of every corner posed its own threat, and when they arrived at a long, empty lot that had to be crossed Mr. Zadian had the party halt. He then whistled and from the ruins of a gray warehouse across the way appeared a small and angular boy leading a pointy headed dog.

The boy answered with a whistle and Mr. Zadian said to John Lourdes, "When we start across do not stop no matter who might fall."

He then whistled again, and the boy kneeled. He had the dog by the neck and he patted him hard then he let the beast loose.

The damn thing took off like a shot across that field with tin cans tied to his neck by long ropes. A wall of gunfire tried to chase that rattle and clang as the dog darted past rubble, his legs moving so they hardly left puffs of dust in their wake.

Mr. Zadian gave the signal and the men sprinted across that open lot, keeping low to the ground and behind the gunfire. When they made the next street there was the dog with a squat fellow in a long coat. The creature's chest was heaving, and damn if he didn't look like he was near ready to have at it again.

Just up from the corner they approached a shed door where armed men stood guard. Mr. Zadian turned to John Lourdes, "Tomorrow . . . people will come and look for the bullets, and we will melt the lead and brass to make our own. That . . . and the dog. What is the word in English to describe these things?"

There was a lot he could have said. Being at the wrong end of the hill, for one. "Improvising," John Lourdes told him.

They entered the building. It was dark except for a light emanating up through a hole in the floor where Mr. Zadian started down a set of rickety stairs. John Lourdes was motioned to go next, then the two men with rifles followed. He found himself in a tunnel tall enough for a man to stand in upright.

The tunnel went off in tangent directions. At the bottom of the stairs was a kerosene lamp that Mr. Zadian picked up. John Lourdes followed him down a hacked-out corridor that had been cut so narrow his shoulders scraped the sides of the tunnel. It was damp, and every time a shell landed nearby the earth shuddered and the men stopped. They stood close around the dusty and trembling light until the dirt seeping from the roof above their heads went still. It was then they resumed breathing and followed the jiggering light into the darkness.

They came to another roughly hammered together stairway and John Lourdes was ushered up it into large room the light filled. It was mud brick, with a second-story loft. There was a table in the room with a lamp on it. About a dozen men, including Malek, sat in chairs or on the floor, or stood with their backs against the wall. Mr. Zadian pointed to the table and offered, "Help yourself."

On the table was *lavash* and cheeses and *gata* bread and wine and cups and a bottle Mr. Zadian held up. "Vodka made from cornel berries . . . If you have such a taste."

"Vodka sounds about right."

They poured him a polite but lethal glass, which he raised in toast. "Gentlemen . . . To your health, and your future."

Mr. Zadian translated. The men nodded, and they raised their glasses.

John Lourdes took a healthy swig of their home brew and the men watched to see how he'd handle it. It had that same clear and wonderful burn that came from hard-core tequila or mescal. John Lourdes wiped his mouth. "Tell your friends here they ought to come to Texas. And bring the recipe."

He put the glass down. He took out a cigarette. He looked at the priest. "Now that the pleasantries are done . . . Let's talk why I'm here."

Mr. Zadian translated. The priest said, "Was I right about him?"

Mr. Zadian continued, "We are members of the Dashnaktsu-tyun—"

"This is about the man who came to see me today at the Mission compound, isn't it?" said John Lourdes.

Again Mr. Zadian translated and the priest said, "Ask him about the American."

"This Mr. Frost . . . is with your government," said Mr. Zadian.

John Lourdes lit his cigarette. "Yes. He requested—"

Malek interrupted Mr. Zadian, who stopped talking and listened then questioned John Lourdes. "You are very different from this official. How is it you were chosen to come here?"

There was a brutal economy to the priest that John Lourdes had experienced in only one other man. He finished his drink, poured more. He smoked. He never once during all that took his eyes from Malek. "I know what you're doing," he said to the priest. "I understand you very, very well. And you don't need me to answer that question. Do you?"

He then raised his glass and drank. Mr. Zadian translated, and the men glanced at the priest. Malek sat in the chair with his arms folded across his lap, and Mr. Zadian said, "Shall I ask him the question again?"

The priest said, "No. He's answered it."

"Mr. Lourdes," said Mr. Zadian, "we want to know if we can . . . work with him."

John Lourdes looked into his near empty cup of vodka. "Where have I heard that before?"

"Excuse me?"

He shook his head. He drank the vodka down. "What kind of berries made this?"

"Cornel."

"It isn't tequila . . . but it's a horserace." He paused. "You want to know . . . what does he want to support your cause?"

"Yes."

"And does he mean what he says?"

"Yes."

"And what can you get?"

"Yes."

"You have more urgent issues. I listen. I hear the Turks fire ten shots, I hear you answer with one. If the Entente can't send a relief column, Van will fall. Maybe not this week . . . but not long after. And you'll be nothing but . . . the deported and the exterminated."

"Where is America in all this? And I'm not speaking of the ambassadors and missionaries. What do we mean here? As people. Do we mean anything?"

How does he explain—resource control. How does he tell men whose families have been thrown into the ocean, tossed from cliff-tops then shot, whose heads were used for target practice about—resource control.

"I don't know why you're asking me. When he knows." He pointed toward the priest with his cup, which he went and filled again. "You know," he said, staring squarely at Malek, "With a man like you it's almost instinctive." He paused momentarily. "I knew another man like that once. But he's dead."

The priest listened, the priest stood. The priest walked up to John Lourdes. The priest poured a cup of vodka. He drank. He looked into the empty cup, his face was weary. He spoke to the others. "If it wasn't for the oil . . . we would not be worth a single grave. They want oil, we a nation. We'll see if either gets what they want."

nineteen

HERE WAS INTENSE street fighting that night within blocks of the American Mission compound. The Turks tried to raze a barricade, but the return fire from a *teerk* crippled the assault. Soldiers were left wounded and dead in the street.

The compound itself was quiet and dark. John Lourdes walked the grounds smoking. He was in conference with himself over cold hard realities. The priest obviously had a plan, and the odds were it would almost certainly be in conflict with whatever Frost had in mind. John Lourdes also understood, he was done. Frost would replace him because he could not be trusted to negotiate veracity.

He passed the church. He glanced in the windows. The moon left soft spill marks upon the floor where children lay bundled up around their mothers like litter pups. Yet, they all slept. Even with the artillery and rifle fire, they slept. For a little while those small, softly breathing bodies were beyond grief and fear and hunger.

He walked up the porch steps. Hain had yet to return. He was almost to the door of his room when the floor boards creaked and a shadow quietly rose up from the darkness.

"Alev?"

She had been sitting on a porch bench.

"I was waiting. To make sure you were all right. You are all right?"

"I'm all right."

"I saw you down by the church."

He looked back. The crown of the roof stood out in the moonlight. "They sleep through the bombing."

"They learn how quickly."

They looked at each other in the bare light of a burning cigarette. She handed him his notebook.

"You have everything?" he said.

"Yes."

He put it back in his vest pocket.

"You write a lot about your father. And why they picked you to send here. I hope it wasn't wrong of me to read that."

"No, Alev. It was not wrong. In fact, I knew you would."

They shared an unspoken moment. He wondered, what thoughts were passing through her mind. She leaned up and without a word put a hand to his cheek, kissing him there. He closed his eyes momentarily. Her presence felt inexhaustible and true.

She told him, "My father used to say . . . every man carries the history of the world in his soul. And, what it means to lose your soul is to lose the world. To lose the world means the poor and the broken and the suffering are nothing to you. They are just an unseemly weight, and the wrongs afflicted against them should be left to others. Your notebook. It tells me you still carry the world in your soul. And I know how difficult that can be."

She went to leave him, but something more came to mind. "In your notebook . . . you wrote 'Harmon Frost' and then . . . 'resource control'?"

John Lourdes ground his cigarette out on the porch post.

"What is . . . resource control?"

"The future," he said.

———

THE NEXT DAY John Lourdes was notified Harmon Frost wanted him at a meeting with the priest. The guide returned with news. He had been on the street the night before and had seen John Lourdes enter the teerk. Later, he had followed the priest and a number of men to the southeastern-most section of the Gardens. There was a small home and barn virtually hidden in a grove of old and bent willows. Hain watched the men squatting around a map on the ground, their faces lit by a kerosene lamp. They were discussing plans for the priest to leave Van.

"Do you know where? Did you hear?" said John Lourdes.

"Russia," said the guide.

About a block from the American consulate, Harmon Frost had set up offices in what was once a tavern. The ground floor was empty and in a miserable state of disrepair. The small rooms on the second floor he had turned into offices. There was an enclosed courtyard at the rear, but a shell had taken down a tall poplar along with part of the wall, and now the tree stretched across the rubbled space and was braced against the building.

A balcony ran along the front of the building from where John Lourdes watched the street and waited on the priest. Members of the Armenian boy scouts, in uniform and under the supervision of their troop leader, searched for the remains of bullets fired the night before. And from the balcony he could look over the roof of a mud shell where crowds of people collected around a public oven in the desperate hope for food.

John Lourdes had been asked to wait alone while Harmon Frost consulted with two field operatives. They were named Van Duyn and Moss. They were about the same age as John Lourdes, well educated and politically savvy. They had questioned him intensely about Malek. He told them much, but he did not offer information about the guide, the meeting at the *teerk*, nor about Russia.

Malek arrived with Mr. Zadian and the dragoman. He still wore the gunbelt. From the balcony John Lourdes raised a hand as a hello. Malek glanced up at him and smiled. He then said something to the others, and they nodded.

All were gathered together in one office. It was bare but for a desk and an assortment of chairs and a table with a samovar from which tea was served. They shared courtesies and tobacco and idle talk. Van Duyn spoke Russian and Turkish, Moss neither. John Lourdes found himself relegated to a station in the doorway, and while he watched the men drink tea and discuss matters of war, he saw Malek move off alone and stare through the open window to the mountains beyond.

For a few secret moments an expression passed over the priest's face that John Lourdes remembered from when Malek stood chained in the prison yard at Erzurum.

Harmon Frost casually called the meeting to order. "Let's discuss our interest and aims."

Mr. Zadian now served as interpreter.

"Your goal," said the priest, "is to help win the war against the Turks. Our goal goes well beyond that.

"Our goals," said Harmon Frost, "are political. We are set upon the sponsoring and spreading of democracy. But our goals are also humanitarian. We are a humanitarian nation. Your survival is important to us."

"It is important, but to be honest, not mandatory."

"Oh, I disagree."

"There are many Armenians in America, in Bulgaria, Greece, in half a dozen other nations, that have pled with the British to form a special unit. To bring them here, train them, arm them. So that they may serve. His Majesty's government has been against that."

"I don't speak for the British."

Mr. Zadian interjected, "Where is the American government in all this?"

"I cannot discuss that."

"Influential Americans have approached your government about helping influence the British to create such a fighting force."

"I cannot discuss that, rather, let's focus on what we can do now."

Mr. Zadian translated for Malek, who waved an arm and went on, "The British are only interested in us in so far as it pertains to the safety of the Suez Canal . . . And the oil fields of Basra. Which the government has control of through companies like British-Persian Petroleum and Dutch Shell, which they clandestinely own and operate."

Mr. Zadian told all this to Harmon Frost, as the priest continued on. "We also know that the British have a secret accord in place with the Entente to divide up Turkey after the war. And that the British intend to take three *vilayets* . . . Mosul, Baghdad, and Basra . . . and create some kind of country out of that. Which is to serve not only as a buffer zone, but a station, where they can politically and militarily keep control of the oil. Where is the American government? What does the American government think of such a plan?"

"Whatever they think," said Harmon Frost, "has not been shared with me. And understand . . . We are not at war with Turkey. We are not one of the allies. We are not privy to all private discussions. So I cannot validate what you said."

"But you do not dispute it?"

"I am neither in a position to validate nor dispute it."

"Yet you want the oil as badly as they do."

Mr. Frost leaned forward and folded his hands on the desk and unflinchingly said, "As badly as we all will."

Frost stood. "Let me summarize. You want to survive. You want to defeat the Turks. You want to build a nation. We can help in certain ways. We can get you weapons . . . food . . . money. Through important business connections, banking channels, charitable organizations, foreign exporters of materials."

"What do you want from us?"

"Create resistance in the south at Mosul. The Turks are intent upon driving to Basra. The British will march north to confront them. We assume they will meet somewhere around Baghdad."

"Is this your plan, or the British?"

"Does it matter?"

"Through our actions," said the priest, "you will buy good will you hope gives you access to the oil fields of Basra from which the British have excluded you."

"The same good will you need to build a nation."

There followed a calculated silence in the room. Then Harmon Frost spoke again, "Mr. Van Duyn and Mr. Moss will work closely with you. They are able men who have the complete confidence of our government. One speaks your language, they understand the cultures."

The priest looked the two young men over. "What about that one?" said the priest, pointing at John Lourdes in the doorway.

"We feel there are other areas where Mr. Lourdes may more ably serve us."

The priest made a slight grunt. He walked up to the two young men and asked about them. Van Duyn explained they were from Harvard and Yale. They had experience in Washington. Their families were diplomats and successful businessmen. With that Malek turned to John Lourdes.

The grim course of an artillery shell gripped the room. It exploded in a nearby street. The building shuddered, the fallen tree scored a few inches down the wall from the quake. The men waited. People could be heard running to the scene. Through the windows smoke began to measure up against the sky.

The priest still stood before Van Duyn and Moss. He turned his attention back to them. "Show me your wounds," he said.

"Excuse me?" said Van Duyn.

"Your wounds . . . show them to me."

Van Duyn explained to Harmon Frost what the priest was asking.

"Show me where you've bled," the priest then said. He ran his hands along the man's suit. "Show me where you've bled for something. For anything."

The two young Americans were at a loss to answer. Malek sat and took off one of his slippers. He showed them the black and dead flesh on the soles of his feet where the nails had been hammered into the bone. He told them in detail the harrowing blow by blow. He then put the slipper back on and stood.

"I need men who speak another kind of language, who understand a far different culture. This one," he aimed a closed fist at John Lourdes, "I know his wounds. I have seen where he bled.

"I do not know you," Malek said to Harmon Frost. "And I do not know these two young men of yours." Again he pointed that fist toward John Lourdes. "That young man. He is the America I know. The America I would put my faith in." He paused, "And I don't want him with me either."

Malek then sat. He spoke privately to the dragoman, and it was the dragoman who continued, "We have people working with us in Constantinople. And we have received word that influential Russians . . . men who are Bolsheviks have met with the German consulate. Men such as yourself, efendi," he said to Harmon Frost, "who are . . . unofficially with their government. And their aim is to let the Germans know that if they back the Bolshevik overthrow of the government, when they attain power, they will immediately sue for peace. Which will remove the Russian from the Turkish flank."

"It would also," said Mr. Zadian, "allow the Turkish army and the German army to sweep across the Middle East. Then they would be able to finish the Berlin to Batum to Baku Railway and the pipeline and so control half the oil in the world. It would ensure the deportation and extermination of every Armenian, every Assyrian, every Christian from here to the Mediterranean." He took a moment. "Are you aware of such meetings?"

"That is something I cannot discuss."

The dragoman translated for the priest. John Lourdes watched as the back of Malek's fingers brushed against the mementoes that hung from the gunbelt. He privately spoke to Mr. Zadian, who asked Harmon Frost, "Might a thinking man, a man such as yourself, see a reason why a country, or a vast company, might prefer Russia to fall? Most of the oil coming to the war is by tanker from the United States. Standard Oil and Shell. Who has wanted to gain control of the Baku oilfields and has not been able to with the present regime? Is it not Standard Oil?"

"Your reasoning is sound, but the facts are incorrect."

The priest stood. He was joined by the dragoman and Mr.

Zadian. "Prove me wrong," said Malek. "Send money to Baku. I am going there to organize Armenians to fight the Germans and Tartars and the Turks who are intent on taking back those oil fields. Help us with that. We will earn each other's good will . . . while these good men around me go about the business of creating a nation."

When they had left the office, Harmon Frost sat back and reflected upon a conversation that had not gone well.

"He's politically astute," said Van Duyn. "I give him that much."

"His reasoning is sound," said Harmon Frost.

"And the facts?" said John Lourdes.

Harmon Frost glared at him, "I know what you're insinuating."

"It seems," said John Lourdes, "the priest understands resource control as well as you."

twenty

*T*HE GUNFIRE HAD intensified dramatically. The guide was sitting by a wall near the public oven bundled up like a tramp so as not to be recognized when the priest left the building. He looked up at the balcony and John Lourdes pointed at both his eyes then clasped his hands together. The guide nodded and was up and working the edges of the crowd to follow Malek.

Harmon Frost called to John Lourdes, and when he returned to the office, Van Duyn and Moss were heading down the stairs.

"Sit," said Harmon Frost. When he heard the tavern door shut he said, "We can't have such things being suggested about us."

"He scared you, didn't he?"

"Being uncertain is one thing, pure distrust quite another."

"Was it his distrust, or his accuracy?"

Harmon Frost sat there, just staring at nothing really. He was unusually subdued.

"The seas of political expediency are about to part."

Harmon Frost turned now his full attention to John Lourdes. Anger flared in his eyes at the remark.

"Resource control," said John Lourdes. "You want me to persuade the priest about Van Duyn and Moss. And Basra."

"Something like that."

John Lourdes told him, "That's not going to happen." He then stood. He took out a cigarette and lit it. "I learned a few things from this meeting." He folded his arms. He let the smoke drift out his nostrils. "Malek is going to Russia. And you know what else." He used the cigarette as a pointer. "Even though the very thought will not be to your liking . . . I'm the one going with him."

ALONG THE LENGTH of the Gardens there was firing. The Turkish strategy was to turn the streets into a turmoil. A shell had landed in the trenches just below the Mission compound wall, and the casualties were being carried on blankets and stretchers up to the hospital. This was in clear violation of Turkish law. The compound could no longer be guaranteed neutrality from enemy fire, and it might well warrant seizure by troops.

Making his way through grey rivers of smoke, John Lourdes found Alev Temple amidst the chaos of the wounded being taken to a place of surgery. Children, swept up with fear, crowded the corridors. For John Lourdes she had only moments to offer.

He took care not to be overheard. "I have been told," he said, "there is a clandestine network of missionaries who plan and execute escapes for those hunted by the government."

She looked around, she was fearful. He took her measure. What he'd asked would put her and others at risk.

John Lourdes waited in the dining room of the doctor's cottage. He had a map spread out on the table he studied. When Alev Temple returned with the doctor's wife, her nurse's smock was stained with blood. She was exceedingly nervous.

"I need to get the priest out of Van," said John Lourdes. He looked down at the map and ran his fingers along the route he hoped to travel. "Can you get us down the Tigris? Possibly to Mosul. Or where we can strike east to the Caspain Sea?"

Mrs. Ulster took a long breath, "Russia."

"Russia," he said.

"Baku. The oil fields," said Alev Temple.

"Can you arrange it?" said John Lourdes.

The doctor's wife covered her mouth and jaw with a hand while she considered, "Alev . . . letter paper and pen, please."

Alev left the room. Mrs. Ulster suddenly remembered, "John . . . a letter was delivered for you last night. Through the British consulate. I hadn't seen you—"

It was on a sideboard and she retrieved it for him.

He was expecting no letter, especially coming through the British consulate. He looked at the envelope. Written there:

John Lourdes
Citizen of Mexico
American Mission compound

He felt something strike at the space in his throat. He opened the envelope. He removed the letter and read:

I have followed you to Van. Saw you through field glasses from Toprak—Kala. I had assumed you would eventually be there at the mission compound.

I await our next meeting. The roads are watched, for I know the priest must be on the move. He spoke to many in the prison about his plans for a nation.

I have one question. Was the araba *part of the original plan to escape the city? Or was it a stroke of ingenuity during dire circumstances? Either way, I have taken notice.*

The British Consul's office was kind enough to deliver this. I will be on the hill at sunset with field glasses, so that we may salute our mutual efforts.

Rittmeister Franke

John Lourdes packed his belongings and waited for the guide to return. At end of day he climbed to the hospital roof. The air was hazy with ash and the streets below a wasteland of bomb craters and smoky plots of brick. The quarter was being taken down piece by piece.

He found the hill with the last of the sun red upon its slopes. The movement of the men could be marked by their long black silhouettes.

He was there, as promised: Rittmeister Franke. By a breast-work where riflemen fired into the Gardens. This time, it was he who tipped his hat.

Why had the captain done this? Was it a vain impulse? Had he meant it as challenge or threat? His father had always cautioned him—keep your eyes at gunsight level. Yet John Lourdes had been caught off guard.

Later that evening the guide returned to the compound and reported to John Lourdes, "Efendi . . . the priest will be on the move tonight."

They prepared for the leaving in John Lourdes' room. He tossed an envelope of lira across the bed. Hain's mercenary wage.

"After you take me to him, our business is done. He and I will go alone."

"But you are not part of his plan."

"I will be."

The mounts were stabled well back in the Gardens. As John Lourdes and the guide walked to the compound gate, John Lourdes unexpectedly stopped.

"Efendi?"

He stared past the entry lamps, the wind tossing their light about the compound walls.

"How difficult would it be," said John Lourdes, "for a Turkish soldier, or a Kurd bandit to disguise himself as an Armenian and wander about the quarter, or watch the compound here, from just outside the gate?"

Hain looked toward the gate, "As easy as the doing."

John Lourdes thought about the captain, the letter. The compound could well be under surveillance.

They removed the dead from the compound in carts. Wrapped in shrouds, and stacked like so much baggage. A canvas tarp was thrown over their remains. The wooden vessel trundled along, pulled by sorry horses from the compound to a place of burial.

By a quiet grove well beyond the range of artillery the cart pulled off the road and two men rose from the dead and stood in the cool night air. John Lourdes looked to make sure they were not followed.

Hain could not free himself from the shroud fast enough. "Efendi?"

"What?"

"I hope to do this only once . . . When it counts."

AT A FARMHOUSE the priest sat alone on a stone wall smoking. Framed by windowlight he seemed to John Lourdes a study in conflict. His horse stood nearby at the ready.

The guide had brought John Lourdes to a cluster of trees along an irrigation ditch close enough to where the priest sat. They spoke in hushed voices.

"You have done well," said John Lourdes.

"Efendi. Russia . . . It will be a hard journey."

"I would believe so."

"I have never taken such a journey," said the guide. "And I have cause to wonder."

THE PRIEST HEARD the slight packing of brush and turned and moving toward him from shadow to shadow was John Lourdes leading his mount. He had the reins in one hand and in the other a bottle of vodka and a tin cup.

The priest bore a look of pure surprise. John Lourdes slipped over the wall and joined him. He set the cup down on the wall. "You'll see, after a drink or two we'll be like . . . old cellmates."

He poured out some vodka.

"I have a map. I'll show you a plan."

He forced the cup into the priest's hand. Some vodka spilled. He apologized and poured more, then carefully touched the tin cup with the bottle. "To the journey."

He drank, the priest could still only stare. John Lourdes took a folded-up map from inside his vest.

"You have no idea," said the priest, "do you, son?"

The priest, of course, knew this young man did not understand. And yet—

John Lourdes set the map on the stone wall. He used the bottle to hold down one end so the breeze could not have at it. He ran his fingers along a route he'd drawn. "You . . . Me . . . Baku."

"I didn't want the others," said the priest, "because I did not trust them."

John Lourdes pointed, "The Tigris . . . We follow the river . . ."

"I didn't want you because . . ." The priest was angry. But not at the young man before him. "I don't want to see you dead."

John Lourdes kept pointing to the map. "Alev says if we get to Mosul from there it's a dead run east to the Caspian Sea, then to Baku."

The priest drank the cup empty, he then tossed the cup aside. He stood. He grabbed John Lourdes' arm. He shoved him away. "You've done enough. You've given enough. Go home!"

John Lourdes pulled loose. He reached out to touch the priest's gunbelt and the lives that hung there. "I understand. Believe me . . . I . . . of all people . . . understand."

The priest took the map forcibly from John Lourdes. He folded it, then stuffed it into the young man's vest and in no uncertain terms demanded he be gone. He spoke angrily, he nearly shouted.

John Lourdes would not be ordered, he would not be overruled, he would not be outmatched. There were men in the house who could now be seen in the windowlight and framed in the doorway as it swung open. They bore arms and came forward quickly. Mr. Zadian and the dragoman among them.

There was movement in the brush behind Malek. He turned. Light sparely reflected off that narrow course of water, and there stood the guide. The priest addressed him.

"What have you heard?"

Hain stood with eyes downcast.

"What have you heard?"

"Everything."

"You will tell your friend here nothing of what I have said. Do you understand?"

He nodded.

"Let there be no mistake."

twenty-one

*T*HE PRIEST WAS overruled. There in the garden beside an irrigation ditch by a committee of men whose futures also hung in the balance.

John Lourdes asked the dragoman for a dozen riders to help him effect Malek's escape from the city. He ordered the mounts' hooves be bound in heavy cloth, the same was to be done to their muzzles. They would leave immediately from the easternmost portal of the city, where there were no barricades, and few guard stations.

The roofs of the town were dark along the streets where they walked their horses. The bindings made them a near silent and ghostlike presence. Where they took to their saddles, the guide pinned an amulet to his blouse. It was a small eye made of brass, painted blue and white, with a black pupil to ward off the *nazar*.

The dragoman saw this and he winked at Malek. He told the guide, "You will need more than one to keep away all the evil that looks down on you. Many more. A treefull, at least."

They emerged from the city single file and following the thread-line of a dried and forgotten irrigation channel. The guide rode at the front of the column. With the moon clouded as it was, it would take more than a watchful eye to pick up the slight dust made by their soundless ponies. But when the guide's hose sniffed at the air uneasily he signaled for the men to halt. John Lourdes came up alongside him. The fires indicating guard stations were few and far between on that plain. The two men watched and listened, stilling even their breath to pick up the slightest hint of a sound.

From across the darkness came the rattle of shots. Flashings just above the reach of the earth. A horse screeched out and reeled into the channel wall. The riders swept up out of that dried waterway. There came a wild and erratic flurry of firing along the plain. Errant flashes everywhere.

The riders were already scattering when a flair rocketed toward the hills and the plain around them burst with light. They and their dust was luminescent as they raced into the landscape.

The escaping horsemen were making for the horizon in groups of two and three. Some toward the Entente armies with letters begging for the relief of Van. Others to Constantinople and Trebi-zond. It was also a means by which, if the Germans knew the priest would attempt to escape the city, they would have to hunt down each pack to have him.

Three of the riders came to a stone ridge and halted. John Lourdes scanned the country they had just traversed with field glasses. The priest and the guide waited beside him.

The city was under heavy bombardment and on the plain he could make out sallies of gunfire chasing down riders, or closing in on men who must have lost their mounts and were fighting it out on foot.

"I heard German being shouted, did you?" said John Lourdes.

"I heard, efendi."

There was something of arguable substance moving in their direction upon the broken terrain. John Lourdes kept watching. It was either the wind taking up the dust along the slopes, or they were being hunted.

⌒

THEY PRESSED ON into the indifferent darkness, halting every few miles and looking back. While the horses rested, another flare took to the heavens.

The priest spoke, and the guide asked, "What does that mean, efendi?"

He had seen this before, he had made this fight once before, with his father. In another country, yes. But its meaning was the same.

"It's a marker," he said. "Either one of the men has been taken and made to talk . . . or we were discovered."

They climbed back into their saddles and prepared for a long and exhausting night. Within an hour another flare burned above the low black hills behind them.

"I have not seen this," said the priest. "Can they hunt that well at night?"

The guide asked, and John Lourdes answered.

"What you are witnessing is a plan. Most of the men on the hunt, are resting somewhere. But they send a small party ahead. They track as best they can. They don't have to get far. Come morning, the ones resting will catch up quickly with the advance party. Then they will take up the pursuit. The ones that hunted during the night will take their turn resting. This way, they are forever on the move. One group resting, one hunting. Pressing. Forcing us to keep on the move. The flares mean to frighten. So we don't sleep. To keep reminding us they are out there."

"Efendi," said Hain, "you know this kind of pursuit?"

"I have been hunted like this before."

Miles later, they watered their horses at a stream. There came the first twitter of birds before the dawn. The earth was cool, and silent. There were no flares, no signs of men. Malek walked up alongside John Lourdes, and together they watched.

"It's not the flares," said John Lourdes, "it's the telegraph. Have they telegraphed on ahead? The German officer. The one in Erzurum. He was also in Van. They interrogated men at the prison in Erzurum. They know what your aims are. That same officer contacted me in Van . . . at the mission." John Lourdes cursed privately. "He is that kind of smart. He will telegraph ahead."

The priest listened soberly as Hain translated and the priest then shook his head, "They will never have us, and how do I know?"

He walked to the guide. He reached out and tugged his blouse below the amulet with its blue and white eye staring imperiously out upon the world. "We are safe from evil. Prince Hain and his magic amulet will protect us."

They pressed on into the Mesopotamian plain toward the head-waters of the Tigris. It was a shadowless country, hard and sweeping save for windswept rock that rose like battlements from nothing. This was country John Lourdes understood. That smelled and tasted and breathed of his home and birth.

They passed a nameless village chiseled into the volcanic flesh of a mountain. Flight upon flight of terraced dwellings such as the pueblos of the west John Lourdes knew from photographs. Their black doorways like empty, dead eyes.

Through the haze a huge crucifix stood guard over the landscape. John Lourdes took out his field glasses. It was a church with a low compound wall squared around it. The building itself was a two-story and windowless structure of mud brick. The cross was of darker stone architected into one of the building walls. But it was the tall stakes bound together that he could not understand. Not until the wind settled some and the images sharpened. They were gallows from which hung children and women and men. Corpses obscured by wind blowing dust through their clothes and bones.

"Efendi," said the guide. "What is there?"

He did not answer. The priest asked for the glasses. John Lourdes did not offer them over.

They rode on, and sometime in the afternoon heard the din of an aeroplane. They pulled up their mounts and looked out upon the wilderness as they waited.

Suddenly a set of pale wings and a propeller brushed over the tips of a far escarpment. It was approaching from the west, from the valley of the Euphrates River. It descended, and as it did, its flight path altered and it set on a course right toward them.

Its shadow struck past so close above, the horses reared and shuddered and dust was pulled up from the earth around them.

"Turkish," said the priest.

"Efendi," said the guide. "I have heard the Germans and the Turks are bringing in planes to scout the British advance up from Basra to Baghdad. And that these aeroplanes are being stationed somewhere along the Euphrates." He pointed to where the aeroplane had first been spotted.

They watched and soon the wings banked and the plane came back toward them. It flew so low now it seemed they could reach up and touch it. When it passed overhead the wind of it blew hard against the men's faces and they could see the pilot clearly, his goggles and great moustache.

Then the aeroplane rose and started away, but not toward where they had first seen it. Now it was traveling in the direction from where the horsemen had come.

"You say they have a military station along the Euphrates?"

"That is what I heard," said the guide.

"Troops?"

"I don't know, efendi."

"If they have a station . . . they may have troops . . . and a telegraph."

In the light of afternoon they ascended a vast plateau. From that height John Lourdes could assess the country before them. While the horses rested, each man took a turn with the field glasses.

As the priest was handed the glasses he said to the guide, "Ask him how he ended up being the one ordered to Russia."

The guide conveyed the question and John Lourdes answered, "I volunteered. So it was decided."

The guide explained.

"Decided how?" said the priest. "The man from the State Department had no intention of ever sending him. That was apparent. What happened after I left?"

The guide asked John Lourdes.

"Upon reflection, he thought I was best equipped."

The guide explained.

The priest set the glasses aside. He studied John Lourdes. "He would not have chosen him, if he were the only one in the world to choose from. So . . . there is another reason. Which means he is lying."

"He says . . . you're a liar."

"I'm a liar?"

"That is what he says . . . not I, efendi. Though it seems to me you have the qualities of a pitiful liar."

"You'd be surprised."

The guide took the glasses now, and John Lourdes asked, "The other night before we left. The priest did a lot of talking. And he said something to you."

"It was nothing, efendi."

"It didn't seem that way to me."

The priest asked, "What is he saying?"

"He wants to know about our conversation at the stone wall."

The priest angered.

"I have not broken honor. I swear it."

John Lourdes picked up on the gaze, the tone.

"Well?"

"Nothing, efendi."

"Nothing?"

"Nothing."

"You're the liar."

"Of course, efendi. But that is a known fact."

"I'm a liar, you're a liar, and he's a liar," said John Lourdes. "We're a matched set."

The priest demanded a translation. He then began to laugh. He called the guide over and whispered in his ear and the guide, at first somewhat shocked, began to laugh. This caused John Lourdes some degree of concern.

"Well?"

"He says we are a family of liars, efendi. He being the husband . . . you, efendi, the wife . . . and I, the illegitimate and idiot child."

The men's laughter was cut short. The guide had picked up something on the horizon and was quick to the glasses.

There was a dark image in the shallows between the sky and the endless timeworn steppes. When the shape rose on the thermals, the guide said simply, "It's back, efendi."

It did not take long, less than a minute, before they picked up the faintest drone of the propeller. The aeroplane was coming straight out of the distance, but at an angle that would take it well to their flank. About two kilometers out, the wings began to bank and the propeller noise grew louder as it headed directly for the plateau.

"Efendi?"

"Let's gather up the horses."

The men quickly went toward their mounts as the plane began to dive and its engine strained and as it swept over them, something was thrown from the cockpit.

twenty-two

HE STICK GRENADE hit about thirty meters from the men. The concussion was enough to throw the guide's mount onto its flanks. It came up shocked and whinnying with the priest grabbing hold of the reins to secure it.

As the pilot banked to make another pass the horseman raced across the plateau like harried game. They spread out to make the killing more difficult. The pilot was only about a dozen meters above them and as that rattling framework passed overhead the pilot leaned from the cockpit and flung another grenade.

John Lourdes saw the tumbling shadow of the thing cross his own just before it exploded somewhere behind him. They made for the slope cradled against the horses' necks and they launched over the side. Their mounts leaned downward and they descended that sandy crag. The aeroplane sped past them overhead in a long whoosh as they made for an island of tall pines.

Once in the timber they dismounted. They looked up through the sheltering light and waited. The flickering image of the enemy passed on overhead, and soon there was another explosion high up in the trees. Shards of timber and stakes with branches and pine needles and flecks of bark rained down on the men. Not long after, the pilot shot off a flare. Sparklers of phosphorous fell through that shadowland of trees.

They held still, breathing hard and listening for what might well come next, when the sound of the engine began to taper off and was soon no more.

THAT EVENING, FROM hills above the Tigris, they saw the lights of their destination.

"Hasankeyf," said the guide.

Before descending the trail to the valley floor they studied the broken terrain they'd come through. Flares had been sent up every few hours, the last answered by a second along a jagged ridgeline that framed the Euphrates Valley.

They were being flanked.

Hasankeyf was a poor town that lay on both sides of the river. It was an ancient settlement that had known the Roman, the Byzantine, and the Arab; it had been sacked by Mongols. Smoke from cooking fires drifted lazily in the windless air above squat, shabby buildings. The moon was clear, and the spire of a minaret on the opposite shore stood before it.

They rode through town on a dirt street muddy from dragged fishnets and pitted by droves of sheep. Across the river where people lived in caves along the cliff face came the shrilly pitch of tin and reeds. John Lourdes could see raven silhouettes around fires at the cavern entry where the musicians played. Their fires, reflecting upon the current, made the Tigris look to be burning.

Hasankeyf was mostly Kurdish so it was left to the guide to barter with an aging beggar to bring them to the home of the missionary known as Zacharias.

He was a small, sickly young man who lived in a pitiful room. He sat at a table holding the letter from Mrs. Ulster close to a kerosene lamp. Upon reading it he said, "Sheepherders have been telling me they've seen troops coming down the Euphrates Valley. And a Turkish aeroplane also to the north."

"It's the priest they're looking for," said John Lourdes.

Zacharias turned to Malek. "Father, it's best then, we leave tonight for Mosul."

"Our horses are pretty ragged," said John Lourdes.

Zacharias stood, "It's all right, John. You see, we'll be traveling by goat bellies."

The missionary was having a little fun at John Lourdes' expense. He led the three men to an abandoned farmhouse along the river a few kilometers north of town where two Turkish boys were preparing a raft by lamplight on a sandy inlet. Zacharias assured them that, the fact the boys were Turkish should be of no concern. He explained they were devout Muslims whose beliefs were not in accord with the actions of the present regime, and were without rancor toward either the Jew, the Kurd, or the Armenian. They were just the poor, struggling to make their way as honest citizens in the world. Then, for John Lourdes, Zacharias went and lifted a goat belly skin from a stack lying beside a kerosene lamp.

The raft being constructed was a *kalek*. These, he told John Lourdes, had been in existence since before the great historian of antiquity, Herodotus, had visited Babylon. A *kalek* was designed for carrying heavy cargo down the dangerous flues and channels of the Tigris.

This raft was to be forty feet long and twenty wide.

Great lengths of pole were set in place with enough space between them for a handful of inflated goat bellies lined up side by side. These were inflated by blowing air through a willow reed, then the skins were sealed shut. They made the *kalek* utterly buoyant. Once rigged in place, a deck was laid over them with smaller poles lashed down by withies.

The raft had been intended for cargo set to be carried downstream. Zacharias explained the situation to the young men, and it was agreed they would leave the cargo, and work through the night to be ready to start downriver with the priest well before dawn.

All pitched in toward that labor. John Lourdes was taught how to inflate the goat bellies then, to sew the openings shut, or bind them closed with cord. He was shown he must wet the skins to keep them from shrinking, or else they would leak.

A gunwale was constructed around the deck to support posts to frame stalls near the bow, for the horses. Their weight would be countered by the men and timbers set in the stern.

⁓

WHEN READY, THEY edged the *kalek* to the shore, easing the bow into the streamy waters. They boarded the horses, who were tentative and shied, and it took patience to get them stabled and tethered in their stalls. John Lourdes was ordered to bring extra skins and tarps to make a tent at the stern.

A *kalek* was guided by two oarsmen, and a stout sweep at the stern for a helmsman to steer. The boys took the oars, Zacharias the helm. And with that, the six set off by lamplight.

They made their way downriver. Beyond a turn, the town appeared. Early fires against the last of night. The first yappings of a dog. Sheep moving through the high grass above the beach.

In the river were two huge columns. The remains of a once great Roman bridge that spanned the Tigris and connected the town. They floated past the footings that were easily greater than the boat and two times as high as a man. The supports rose from there. The inlaid stone ascending stories.

They floated on. The water echoed softly as it slapped the footings. On the shore fisherman prepared their nets to be cast upon the waters.

John Lourdes stood at the edge of their craft and doffed his hat. The fisherman looked at this strange man, their expressions unsure.

A feeling came over him, it came like a quiet tide. He was on the Tigris. In that place known as the origin of man. A spiritual homeland for much of the known world. He looked up at the austere remains of that bridge. At the spans that still stood on the opposing shores. At the minaret with the blue light of coming day to shape it. He looked to the fishermen along the beach casting their nets upon the water as had the Apostles.

It was a feeling he had never experienced at home, for America was too young and too far away. The feeling was one of eternity. What Alev Temple had said, quoting her father—each man carries the history of the world in his soul—seemed utterly true. Profoundly and mysteriously so.

And of all things, he could suddenly feel his father's voice, and his mother standing quietly beside him. He was still holding his hat, and looking at it, realized he doffed it as had his father endless times. The pull of his parents became so strong at that moment, it seemed as if they were reaching out from the headwaters of time, touching his every thought, his every word, every deed.

"Efendi . . . there is trouble."

John Lourdes turned.

Soldiers were walking the streets with lanterns. Cavalry were heading up and downstream in the cool dawn light. Others were searching a bluff above the Tigris. Hain pointed towards a sheep path through the high grass just back from the embankment. The three had ridden there to the house where Zacharias lived. On that path scouts were squatting over what could only be their horse tracks and talking among themselves.

John Lourdes addressed Zacharias at the helm. "They will eventually go to where you live. And then upriver to the place the boat was launched."

"If that is God's will."

"Can they catch us by keeping to the shore?"

"There are cliffs . . . jungles of reeds . . . gorges . . . and the current is very strong." He paused. "Their horses will tire, their men will tire. But the Hiddekel, the Great River, never tires."

John Lourdes quietly accepted that, but he looked to the sky.

twenty-three

THEY WERE TRAVELING at five kilometers an hour, and they had come many hours. The country they passed through was untouched, silent, and vast. Miles of marsh reeds gave way to cratered chasms, which gave way to runs of white desert.

The men talked, the men laughed. The priest learned to work the helm. Hain put in time at the oars, singing when not complaining. By unanimous agreement, he was wretched at both. John Lourdes was left to watch.

He watched the sky through his field glasses, he watched the country behind him. He traced every distant marking, each abstract and unsure sign, and no blemish, no aberration, nothing upon the physical architecture of that world escaped his hunting eye. For he understood—the present is uncertain, and the future too far away.

He had been sitting all the while on a crate in the stern, Malek squatting near him at the helm. John Lourdes saw the priest rise and cup a hand over his eyes. The expression on his face changed, and what it changed to foretold the worst. The boys began talking excitedly. There was no misunderstanding their tone, as it matched the priest's stare. John Lourdes came about and stood. He was the last to see.

At that time of the year, melting snow from the mountains caused the river to run high. They had just come through a narrow gorge, where the current funneled and picked up force. But once beyond, the Tigris widened and flattened out, and would flood up the low shoreline before it rushed on. It was not unusual, during those spring months, to find debris strewn along the muddy embankments. But what had been cast there, was not debris.

There were bodies. As far as one could see. On both shores. But these were not just bodies. These were mummified corpses bathed in mud that had dried and caked.

They were not real somehow. Not people, not human beings. These were sculptures. Pieces created by some mad phenomena. Posed masks of sedentated earth. They had to be.

The *kalek* drifted down through this causeway past corpses skewered by tree limbs, corpses that had been roped and gagged, that had been bound together in pairs. Others were frozen in alien or unimaginable positions and the numbers were beyond the possibility of comprehension. There were pyres of dead washed up on the embankment and along white spots of sand, and where the wind blew through the high reeds far back from the shoreline more dead lay in heaps.

Yet it was the silence. The silence there bore a horrific gravity. For this was a cemetery of barbaric measures, a graveyard to vengeance and hatred. These dead had been cast into the unknown, beyond grief and mourning.

On the raft, none dared speak. They just worked the oars and the helm and they looked. And looked.

The priest went and sat on the crate. The current pulled them steadily downriver. There were gulls along the shore. White and beautiful. The dead to them were nothing. Just a momentary place to roost, an obstacle to get around. The priest began to speak. To no one, to anyone, to himself:

"How often does one hear or say . . . They are dangerous people . . . They are tribal and cannot be trusted . . . Their food and ways are foul . . . They are ignorant . . . They mean to steal our world . . . They mean to have us gone from the earth . . . They cheat and lie . . . They are criminal . . . They will defile that which is dear . . . The true god does not reside within their souls . . . They are violent . . ." He paused, "Did such beliefs cause all of this? No . . . they did not. All men are consumed with finding someone else culpable for their own pathetic state of affairs. All men look for someone to blame for their own despair. Someone they can rain down hate and violence on, to exorcise that which has them chained. I know. In the church I killed the soldier . . . revealing how I, too, am capable of all this we see. And the man most vulnerable creating all this, is the man who believes he is not capable of this at all. Who only sees his cause as always right and just." He paused again. "I was taught . . . the path of logic, is the path of folly. Life cannot be reconciled, only recognized. I did not believe it, till I became it."

They coursed down through a wild valley. The river there narrow, the current quick. The shore was marsh with silty water and tall reeds that bent like surrey whips in an unceasing wind. Down the length of that passage those reeds made a bristly and undulating music that covered the sound of a propeller, till it swept forth from a pass in the scrubby foothills the river wound through.

They barely had time to arm themselves. John Lourdes passed his shotgun to the priest as he commanded the guide, "Tell him. At all costs. The plane must be brought down."

They managed to get off a first volley. There were tiny bursts of smoke along the fuselage as the plane made a run overhead. The strains on the struts and tension wires along the wings from the wind caused it to shudder and roll and the first grenade the pilot flung exploded on the embankment and sent up an umbrella of silt and shorn reeds. The aeroplane swooped in for another pass, but this time at a sharp angle to the river to minimize the effect of the wind. It was late noon, the sun shone brightly off the river. John Lourdes had taken from his satchel the flare gun and loaded it.

The plane rattled violently as it rushed over. This time the grenade flung must have been a tin with a rope timer because it blew in the air above the raft, raining down metal screws and nails that raked the deck.

The horses had begun to kick at their paltry stalls. One of the boys took to praying out loud; the other abandoned his oar. The raft started to pull hard to port, and the helmsman got to his knees to hold tight to the rudder as best he could.

The pilot proceeded to come in so low the reeds beneath flattened out. On board the men were putting up a wall of gunfire. Shells caromed off the deck. John Lourdes rested the flare gun on the stall to keep it steady it as the *kalek* pitched and turned.

The flare he fired off, whistled through the wings and hit the fuselage then the tailplane, and burst. There were sparks around the cockpit and the tail shimmied. The plane swerved forcing the pilot to work the lifts to keep from crashing. But even as the shadow of the warplane reeled away the pilot managed another grenade. It came toward the raft with deadly accuracy and detonated just above the waterline beside the boy still at the oar.

Bits of tin and metal tore into his body; the concussion threw him across the deck. Part of the oar impaled itself in the gunwale. The boy lay on the lashings as the priest knelt over him. Grenade fragments had gone through his robe and flesh like hot irons, and there came from him one soundless breath as he died.

John Lourdes grabbed the other boy and tried to get him back to the one oar left. He shook and pleaded with him as Zacharias could not brace against the current alone.

"Efendi . . ." the guide was wrapping a cloth around his badly burned and wounded arm. "Fire!"

There was a trailing of gray streamer upon the sky. The tailplane was smoking. The pilot was in a long bank sighting up for another run.

The boy was held to the oar till he calmed enough to understand his fate at that moment. The pilot was turning toward the river. John Lourdes reloaded his flare gun. The priest had run out of ammunition. The guide rested his rifle in the crease of his bandaged arm as he chambered more rounds.

The men stopped momentarily as the pilot started straight down the Tigris. So close to the river's surface was he, the water flumed up white. The fuselage lifted suddenly, then dropped as thin runnels of fire shot out from the lifts.

The warplane had been hit. The pilot was doing all he could to keep from having to ditch. John Lourdes swung the Enfield from his shoulder and passed it to the priest. Smoke began to billow out from the tail. The pilot was engulfed in smoke, the plane was near touching the river.

The men fired into the heat of that engine. The flare John

Lourdes shot off strafed the wing, then continued out over the Tigris in a blaze line of sparks. The plane was about eighty meters out when the tail snapped and boomeranged into the marshes shredding a pathway of silt. The engine whined, the front end hit the water.

It was a catastrophe of collapsing wood and metal and wire. One set of wings cut the waterline and tore loose. The frame and remaining set of wings skimmed the Tigris like a stone toward that turning raft.

The men threw themselves on the deck as the other wings ripped from the frame and the fuselage rose up with the engine in flames and the propeller still at full throttle. The engine began to burn and black smoke poured forth, and the wings hit the *kalek* and took the helmsman and part of the rudder right on into the river.

The propeller broke loose from its mounting and carried like a pinwheel toward shore hacking through marsh grass and bracken then was gone up over the embankment. The frame flipped past the raft, then flipped again, and the rimpled water in its wake steamed from the burning engine, and the frame speared bottom and came upright like a pylon and the *kalek* hit it with the full measure of force.

The frame came apart. A section from the engine to the remains of the cockpit slammed down on the deck and the sheer weight of it along the stern caused water to pour up over the gunwale by the shattered helm. As the bow lifted, the horses kicked and cried out in confusion, and a stall gate broke loose. One of the mounts went skittering backwards and toppled over the stern and into the Tigris.

The propeller mount was still winding out and scorching the deck beams and the priest took hold of the frame at the far end. He got his hands up under the belly of it, and clasping them together, began to lift.

He managed a few tortured inches, then John Lourdes had the guide slip his rifle under the wreckage. Taking hold of the barrel, they used the weapon as a brace. Water slopped up over their ankles. The men began to exhaust, their muscles weaken. But when they got the frame high enough the priest turned and took the weight of it upon his back. John Lourdes had the guide let loose of the rifle and the men got themselves stationed on the priest's flanks. With what was left of their strength they started to lift again. Their chests heaved, their mouths hung open. But when they had the frame lifted high enough, when the angle was right enough, the weight of the engine dragged the rest of the fuselage down into the gunwale. It cracked apart and the engine took the rest over the side, and as the water closed up over the remains of that warplane the raft settled.

PART III

The Land
of Eternal Fire

twenty-four

THE NIGHT OF the escape from Van, Alev Temple and a hospital aide took a wagon across the Gardens to the Zadian home. It was there the priest had been hidden, and from there the men left from that evening. She anticipated finding wounded and dead, hence the wagon.

The dragoman had news to report, and it was not good. It was his mount that had been shot during the surprise attack. Alone and on foot, with only a pistol, he had managed to make his way along myriad gullies back to the safety of the Quarter.

He had seen and heard much hiding in the darkness. A number of men had been killed or quickly captured. The prisoners taken to a place in the road where they were beaten mercilessly with trench clubs, then repeatedly bayoneted. When these violations were completed, the soldiers doused the bodies with kerosene and set them on fire. All except for Mr. Zadian.

He had been slightly wounded and taken alive. When his wife heard this she began to wail and tear at her clothes, for she knew that by now he would be in a stone and windowless cell waiting to face his interrogators.

About the fate of Malek and the American with him, the dragoman was not certain. He only knew they were not among the wounded and dead that were lying out there on the road.

Even with her credentials, and having a mission aide along, Alev Temple was not permitted to retrieve the dead. They were to be left there as a punitive reminder.

Van was under a heightened security. Many more troops, and more gendarmerie than she had ever seen. There were even roving gangs of Kurdish bandits on patrol. It was now virtually impossible to enter or exit the city, which is why the dragoman approached her the next day at the compound.

He sat on the hospital steps and explained to Alev that Mr. Zadian had been the one assigned to go to Baku and meet with the Armenian resistance in the hills coordinating them, the priest, and the shipments of arms and money. If Mr. Zadian were to be taken or killed, that responsibility fell to the dragoman.

Alev Temple understood why he had come to her. Escaping Van would require considerable and determined planning, and her involvement in this clandestine effort was imperative.

Behind the American consulate was a barn that had been turned into a bar. It was a place for Americans and other foreigners to dull the brutality that constantly besieged them.

Carson Ammons, the newspaperman who had been with her at the death scene on the Bashkale Road, was well into his whiskey when Alev Temple arrived. She asked to sit somewhere where no one could eavesdrop.

"I think I can offer you a very promising story."

"I still have unprintable photographs from your last promising story."

"You'll get to use them . . . The world will see to it."

"I can't cash the future. What do you have for now?

"Malek," she said.

"The priest?"

"Yes."

"Word is he escaped Van."

"He did."

"And so?"

"I have put together papers for a relief mission. With authorization to take a photographer with me. A third man will be coming who will serve as a porter. I have his papers also. This man is to be a conduit . . . between Armenian insurrectionists . . . Malek . . . and a foreign citizen who is delivering to them weapons and money."

Carson Ammons considered this information while he studied the source.

"Would I have the right to do this story? I mean the written story?"

"Who else will be there, but you?"

"This is not the usual province of relief workers."

She answered with her silence.

"Where are we going?"

"Baku."

"Russia?"

———

WHY HADN'T THE pilot returned to report sighting the priest on the Tigris before embarking upon his assault. It would have been the right military procedure, under the circumstances.

John Lourdes kept trying to make sense of it all, as they worked to dock the *kalek* on a sandbar so as to make repairs. The current had carried Zacharias into the marsh grass where they found him unconscious. He had suffered two fractured legs that needed splinting. The mount that had gone overboard the guide retrieved from the Tigris, unhurt.

By dusk, they resumed their journey downriver. The boy and the guide at the oars, Malek at a mended helm. Silent and grave over questions that plagued him, John Lourdes maintained watch. But it proved unnecessary. The hours downriver went without incident, which only magnified a pervasive sense of dread.

There is too much calm—he wrote in his notebook. *Could it speak not to our success at eluding the captain, but rather to some unaccounted for failure on my part, in planning.*

They came within sight of Mosul in the evening hours. The fading light portrayed a formal pattern of streets far into the desert on both sides of the river. There were many rafts upon the shore, many boats with their triangular sails buoyed in the shallows. Men congregated around fires, and women filled great jugs from the river. They came to shore near a bridge. It was, in fact, a roadway built on a trusswork of boats with arced prows. Under torchlight soldiers marched to the eastern shore. The bridge was glutted with men and wagons, with caravans and traders, even at that hour. From the raft they could hear people along the bridge speaking Arabic dialects so they were careful to remain quiet and inconspicuous as possible, for they were in the heart of a place that would show them no mercy.

Zacharias had composed a letter to a missionary by the name of von Ludendorf. He was a distant cousin by marriage of a prominent officer in the German high command.

Bearing this letter, John Lourdes and the guide were led from the mission compound to an Arab coffee house where von Luden-dorf passed the hours. He was a thick-faced, thick-bodied man who looked much older than his forty years. He had come to missionary work by way of his failure at the seminary, his failure at business, his failure at marriage, and his failure at life. Of all this he spoke freely and often, as he took the three by wagon to Persia.

He was loud, well-liked, and held his liquor admirably, and among the Arabs, Turks, or Germans his heritage and status made him one of them, and so he could traverse everywhere easily. He admitted his work in the underground movement was less of a cause than a means to settle a grievance with a world that knew him as a failure.

In the back of the wagon John Lourdes wrote in his notebook—*the virtueless intentions that drive men to virtuous acts.* Was that not, he thought, his own reaction to a comment from a State Department official as to why he was sent to this place.

He looked out through the canvas opening, past their mounts, which were tethered to the rear of the wagon. All the passing miles could not kill the feeling he had somehow failed in the planning of their escape. Flicking the pages of his notebook indiscriminately with his thumb, he noticed the last vestige of a page that had been torn off. On that page Zacharias had written his note to the mis-sionary von Ludendorf.

Suddenly, his mind went through a succession of phantom steps that took him to the answer: The letter . . . The one Mrs. Ulster had written to Zacharias . . . The one he'd read in his room, sitting at the table and holding it near the kerosene lamp. Had Zacharias taken it? Had he left it on the table? John Lourdes could not remember. But if it had been left on the table . . . And there was no way of asking him now, if he had . . . If Rittmeister Franke entered that room . . . If he walked that room . . . searched that room . . . read that letter . . . He would know their destination.

FROM A RIDGE above the desert floor they looked out upon the road that marked the passage into Persia. From that promontory they were on their own. The missionary was turning north toward the town of Amadia. He had received correspondence detailing persecutions there of the Christian and Jew alike, and of rumors Armenians had been left to die in the desert.

They camped that night in the ruins of a palace with a view to the world below. The wind brought with it great veils of sand and the battlements were as nothing against it. The three sat around a fire with their mounts close by in what had once been a grand hall. But its high and expansive archways now shouldered a roofless dome, and the columns that lined the walls were decorated with epochs lost to time.

A troubled John Lourdes revealed his concerns about the letter and what he presumed was a failure on his part that could be endangering them all. The guide translated and the priest listened, glancing occasionally at the bare pieces of brush that burned there in a firepit.

"Tigziz," he said. "Look where you are. Then speak to me of failure."

That next day, by any calculation, John Lourdes would have sworn what he was staring at was some trick of nature being played out upon an anonymous landscape. The others took their turn with the field glasses, and they too could not explain what seemed some immense carpet stitched together from myriad sections of cloth stretching across a sunburned and sand basin.

It took a few kilometers for them to realize it was a tent city in a quarter of the world where no tent city belonged. They passed broken carts hacked down for wood and abandoned valuables still bound up in shawls, they passed the bones of mules that had been skinned and eaten, and other bones yet that belonged in graves. What they rode into was the final solution as underwritten by man.

The emaciated stares that watched the riders belonged to women, and the starved and sickly eyes their children. None moved from the shadow of their tents as the horseman passed. They had so little strength to fight the sun, and how could they be sure these men did not mean them ill or harm. Until the priest dismounted, and praying aloud, walked among them.

These were souls resigned to death, for whom the final moment would be a mercy. Condemned to this place they came forth and reached out to touch the hem of his garment as if some measure of peace and salvation resided there. A woman must have known Malek, for she called out his name and began to pass his story from person to person. The commotion brought other women from other tents with children who were just packages of bone that saw and breathed but did not speak.

John Lourdes watched all this from the saddle as Malek walked the camp with the guide following along behind him and leading both their mounts. The priest clasped the hands of the women who reached out to him, who stood by their tents, who walked the sun alongside his shadow. For those too broken or old, for those who were only husks of paper flesh, he went to them and kneeled, and he held them and he prayed with them, and this too he did with the children. Children who did not understand their plight, who did not deserve this fate, who had been cheated of the barest hours and now had hardly a ghost left in them. He stroked their faces and he kissed their cheeks and he held their frail hands as he whispered in their ears, and he had the guide bring a skin of water, and with this he washed their faces and he wet their tongues. John Lourdes saw the priest allowed neither agony nor rage to have at his features. He was resolve and compassion, moral order and solace. He embodied, thought John Lourdes, the strengths of eternity. And unlike most men, he was unafraid of suffering.

There in the middle of that forsaken camp the priest undid the gunbelt. He held the holster high for all to see. He kept it so, and turned as he began to speak.

"Do you see what this is? I took it from a soldier who meant to see us dead. A soldier to whom we are nothing. Do you see what hangs from this gunbelt? Do you recognize what hangs from this gunbelt?" He turned slowly and he raised his other hand and held the gunbelt between them. "Our ceremonies hang from this belt. Our rituals hang from this belt. Dreams hang from this belt. Joys hang from this belt. Beliefs . . . hopes . . . memories . . . birthdays . . . marriages . . . memorials . . . our religion . . . What hangs from this belt is our history. Can you see? Can you?"

He looked into faces for whom there was no earthly reward. "We are not finished as a people . . . I promise you. You will not be forsaken . . . I promise you. I will bear witness . . . These men with me will bear witness . . . There are others now who will bear witness. A nation will be built on our dying. Our dying. A future will bear your name. A nation will be born of your suffering. Those who come later will know they owe you for your courage. And it will be you who will stand together at Abraham's Tent to greet generations." He took the gunbelt in one hand, and he shook it. "I promise . . . I, and others with me, will put thunder to your rain."

A hobbling woman emerged from the crowd to offer her prayer beads. She asked the priest if he would please add them to the belt. It caught him by surprise, and so momentarily he just stood there before putting out his hand. She set this possession in his palm. He gripped it and he kissed the woman and another woman walked forward with a cameo, and so it was that another moved from the shadows of a tent and in no time there were women all around the priest for him to take something of the life that offered it.

Hain saw the priest was being overwhelmed, and he went to the sack that hung from Malek's saddle and retrieved the stolen chalice. He hurried over and the priest saw what the guide was carrying and he thanked him and he poured a handful of peoples' lives into that cup then he walked the camp with the vessel ever filling.

Women, in their desperation, began to crowd the guide and John Lourdes, who were following behind Malek. They began handing over to these strangers something of themselves.

They spoke to John Lourdes. What they said he did not understand, but this event was beyond the boundary of words. He took off his hat and leaned from the saddle holding it out. It began to fill . . . A handmade rosary . . . A mass card on a string . . . The portrait of a family in a tiny glass bauble . . .

A woman carried her dying son to John Lourdes. The boy had in his hand something he wanted to pass on, but was too weak. John Lourdes leaned out further from the saddle and put out his hand by the boy's. The hand opened and from it fell a tiny crucifix of carved wood, with one cross beam that was in part broken off.

It rested there in his palm. This cross so like one John Lourdes had worn with its own partly broken beam. He looked into a stare at the edge of the abyss resting upon a mother's breast. Here was a boy John Lourdes had never seen before and never would again.

A boy who he could not share a word with, in a death camp, in the desert, somewhere within the Ottoman Empire, who on that day, in that place, had handed John Lourdes back what felt like a part of his own life. A life that had, in part, been lost to him.

John Lourdes closed his fist, and he held that fist to his heart so the boy could see, and the boy's eyes moved ever so slightly as John Lourdes placed the cross in his hat.

twenty-five

HE PRIEST DID not speak, he did not eat. He sat alone in the sand before the Caspian Sea. Beside him on a blanket were those keepsakes that had been passed over to him at the tent camp. In his hands was a scarred bandoleer. John Lourdes and the guide watched as he emptied the bullet rings and then, one by one, he strung and tied then hung each momento from the leather loops. When done he slipped this creation over his head and then slung an arm through the opening so it draped across his chest. He stood and removed his slippers letting the white sand lap around his bare feet.

They were following the coastline north. Terns and gulls broke across the sky with their fleeting calls. Soon the riders came upon the signs of oil. Slicks of it carried on the backs of waves left the shoreline stained and spattered black.

The first sighting of Baku was a slender stylus of flame they rode toward most of the night. They would come to learn it was an oilwell that had been sabotaged. Baku had been taken and retaken since the war began and was now under the control of Russia. It was a place of racial hatred and conspiracies, labor unrest and Bolsheviks systematically plotting to overthrow the government.

They entered Baku through the Icheri Sheher—the old city. Their destination an address along the Alexander Quay. Baku had been built on crude, and there were theaters and concert halls and museums and churches and mansions copied from the arts of Europe and Arabia to match the greed of men anywhere. There were also alleys and vacant lots and gullies of trash where the poor lived in crates and ate dog.

Unshaven and filthy the three traveled the harbor thoroughfare where fleets of oil tankers were being filled and readied to sail. There was smoke across the moon from the well fire, and the air stank with the grit of crude being distilled just beyond the rooftops in the refineries at Cherni Gorod—or Black Town, as the Europeans called it.

The buildings on the block they were searching out were fronted with shops along the street, their windows above stenciled with the gaudy letters of the businesses housed there or with laundry draped down from the sills.

As a precaution John Lourdes thought it best Malek wait, the guide remaining with him, while he went on ahead. They dismounted a street shy of their destination and they led their horses into an alley. John Lourdes left them there and went ahead on foot.

The apartment he was looking for was a walkup. The odor of years permeated the weathered halls. The third floor landing was dingy and dark. Behind the shabby apartment door where he knocked came faintly discernable footsteps. Yet, no one spoke, nothing was said.

John Lourdes knocked again. "Mr. Zadian . . . it's John Lourdes."

The door was unlocked and opened quickly. It was the dragoman with a revolver in hand.

"John . . . finally."

He was barely in before the door slammed shut behind him and locked. The dragoman started across the room. It was a rather drab apartment lit by a single candle. The shut tight drapes made it dusty and claustrophobic.

"Is Malek all right?"

"I thought it best for him and Hain to wait down the street while I came here first."

The dragoman pressed close to the wall and peeled the drape back just a bit. He was distressed, severely so. John Lourdes saw the gun in the old man's hand shook.

"Did you see anyone on the quay that aroused your suspicions?"

"No," said John Lourdes. "Where is Mr. Zadian?"

"Are you certain?"

"As certain as I could be. I came in quick. What's wrong?"

"Zadian was shot during the escape from Van."

"Killed?"

"Wounded. He was taken to the prison on the Citadel . . . for interrogation."

"You know that for a fact?"

"It was my horse shot in the canal."

"I didn't know."

"I made it back to Van by keeping to the irrigation ditches. I saw the others they wounded. And killed. They burned them all in the road. Except Zadian." He paused, then hurriedly closed back the drape. "Put the candle out. Then come here."

John Lourdes snuffed out the flame. He came up behind the dragoman. The old man's breathing had quickened. He opened the drape enough so John Lourdes could see.

"Look . . . Is there anyone that arouses your suspicions?"

There were taverns facing the harbor, and neighborhood cafés, docked ships, drays, so there was no shortage of human traffic to arouse one's suspicion.

"The contact for the munitions and money who was to meet Zadian here," whispered the dragoman, "has never arrived."

John Lourdes turned.

"I've waited two days. That's why—" He pointed to the street.

John Lourdes closed the drape.

"I haven't been out of here once. I listen at the door. I watch. No one comes."

John Lourdes crossed the room. He took off his hat and set it on the desk by the candle. A thin band of smoke rose from the wick. This had the makings of an unmistakable catastrophe.

"How did you get out . . . of Van?"

"The night of the escape, Alev came to Mr. Zadian's home with a wagon. She knew there would be casualties. I thought to ask her."

The dragoman sat in a worn chair. He kept staring at the window. "They know we're here."

"How did Alev arrange it?"

"She and a newspaperman. They requested papers for a relief story. I was to be their porter."

"You left from the mission compound, I suppose."

"You're asking all this for a reason?"

"I believe the compound was under surveillance."

The dragoman looked the picture of defeat. "I have lost all my family. And now this."

"Where is Alev," said John Lourdes.

"At the hotel . . . The Europa." He then pointed his weapon toward the window. "John, something has gone wrong."

twenty-six

THE DRAGOMAN LEFT the apartment and started up the quay. He kept a good pace afoot, but nothing to arouse suspicion or draw attention to himself. At the corner he was to turn up into a thoroughfare with its streetcars and sidewalk cafés where the neatly attired drank beneath the rosy glow of streetlamps. He never looked back. He was to continue on to a park about two streets away, exactly as John Lourdes had plotted.

John Lourdes had left the apartment about a half hour before, through a basement door that opened onto a cart path at the rear of the walkup. To reach the park the dragoman had to pass an outdoor beer garden. There, he pushed aside a caped and filthy drunk who tried to beg for money.

To enter the deeply wooded park one passed through stone gates. The nightwind blew long branch shadows across an empty footpath. The dragoman was intensely wary, and when something stepped from the thicket, he startled.

It was John Lourdes, who took him by the arm and pulled him from the path. Among the deeper reaches of the trees they waited in silence. As only slivers of moonlight filtered through the branches they could not see very far back along the footpath.

A deep quiet settled in that grew more disquieting by the minute. The occasional rustling of leaves and nothing more. Until the sudden and jolting report of gunfire, the flashings from a pistol barrel that momentarily lit the trees.

John Lourdes pulled hard on his companion's arm. "We're going now. And be quick!"

ON A STREET corner at the far end of the park the priest waited with the horses. When John Lourdes and the dragoman arrived, he said, "I heard shots."

Moments later a caped and hooded figure came sprinting down the footpath and out the park gate. It was the guide, who the dragoman now realized was the tramp begging outside the tavern. Hain grinned at the dragoman wickedly while pointing at his own eyes.

"Well," said John Lourdes. "How many were following?"

Hain raised two fingers and tossed John Lourdes a set of wallets. "Turkish officers."

They retrieved the dragoman's mount from where he had it stabled and he led them up through Black City toward the Baladzhary Station. Huge derricks crowded together across the night-sky. Their steel-plated outlines titanic and black upon the horizon. The well fire still burned furiously to the east, and the country around it glowed like the open grate of a furnace. They rode through spills of oil that slopped up around the legs of their ponies and along foundry row the dragoman reined into a wagonpath that led to a stockade. Above the timber gates a sign read:

ORDINA IRONWORKS

A watchman called to them through a small opening in the wall. The dragoman answered, "Tell Mr. Ordina . . . Malek is here."

Minutes later the timber gate eased open on its heavy iron hinges, and the guard, with rifle in hand, stood back and pointed to an office along the palisade wall.

In the light of an open door sat a man in a wheelchair. Mr. Ordina was near sixty and had lost both legs and parts of fingers in the Russo-Turkish war of 1877. He invited the men to follow him into his office.

It was a clutter of desks and cabinets and a table crowded with liquor bottles and beer. Mr. Ordina had a driving physicality about him that belied his crippled state, and he wanted to know everything of the priest's journey from Erzurum to that evening in the streets of Baku. But John Lourdes was quick and clear, there were urgent matters to contend with.

The contact had not arrived. There were no funds, no munitions. And no word, no explanation, no reason. John Lourdes prepared an urgent dispatch in code for Harmon Frost. One of Mr. Ordina's most trusted men carried it by motorcycle to the telegraph office in Black City. But time would be the enemy to their determination of will.

"Gentlemen," said Mr. Ordina, "all is not without hope."

A KEROSENE LAMP flared over a meager supply of munitions in a darkened shed at the rear of the ironworks. Older rifles, cartridges of inconsistent caliber. At least there was dynamite, and a handful of grenade rifles.

"I've been building up my own arsenal," said Mr. Ordina. "For when the revolution comes, and the Bolsheviks try and rob me of all I worked for."

John Lourdes looked over those few instruments of war. The measure of so little, that was meant to carry the day.

The smell of the wood casings, the packing, the straw and paraffin and lubricant caused John Lourdes to flash on the oil fields of Tampico just nights before his father's death. The ever-increasing presence of his father became for him near too much to bear. A man he'd hated and fought, was utterly and absolutely alive in the half life of the moment.

Armenian irregulars were camped in the hills waiting for Malek and the munitions. There was a barracks hut within the compound Mr. Ordina had intentionally left empty, so when Malek and those with him arrived they would have a safe place to rest and wash and prepare.

After ridding himself of weeks of road filth John Lourdes lay down to rest, but sleep did not come. Before dawn he rose as men arrived for work, and he discovered a stairwell to the foundry roof from where he could look out upon the peninsula of the Baku.

It was a world beyond anything he had experienced in the oilfields of Tampico. Here was the limitless economy of destruction stretching inexhaustibly from horizon to horizon. Derricks encased in iron slating for protection against fire were buttressed to each other like an interconnected network of endless steel and wood rigging, with great brick stacks smoking in the gold of first light. There were spills of oil around derricks, spills that created rivers following the contours of the earth, spills the size of ponds, the breadth of lakes. And everywhere debris, everywhere garbage, endless cable and masses of iron and metal left to rot and rust in the sun for so long, roads had been built to go around them.

While staring upon that vast construct, he came to realize why he had not been able to rest a while ago, and why his father's presence had been so real and overwhelming in that shed. With clear and precise emotions, he came to understand the driving force behind that which brought him to this place.

And it was not that it shocked him, for it was a true account of all that he was. But that the revelation had come precisely now, and it was as simple as a single word.

ONE HUNDRED AND fifty Armenian volunteers were living alongside a quarry owned by the Ordina Ironworks. They existed in tents and huts patched together with scrap and mud plaster. The priest arrived with one wagon bearing the sparse munitions. The volunteers stood like nervous spectators staring at him. Stepping from the saddle, Malek put out his hands and spoke, "Am I not among friends and patriots?" With that, John Lourdes watched as the volunteers crowded up around Malek bowing, many wept openly, and as always, the priest greeted each man as if a brother from birth.

When a moment allowed, John Lourdes took Hain and the priest aside so they might speak privately, "Tell him . . . I'm going to meet with the German."

The guide hesitated. "Efendi?"

"You'll be coming with me."

The guide explained to Malek, who responded, "How will you know how to find him?"

"I already know."

The guide told this to the priest, who answered immediately, "It was foolish of me to ask when I was certain of the answer." The priest was concerned. "A confrontation is inevitable. Better now."

John Lourdes, it seemed, had more to say. The priest saw and spoke to the guide. The guide said, "He sees there is something else on your mind."

"I learned something," said John Lourdes, "through coming here that made me able to convince Harmon Frost I was the one to do this. What I learned is . . . the people who sent me don't like outsiders. They are uncomfortable going to people outside their small group. Even though they chose me because I look like an outsider. Because I look "not white." I have Mexican blood in me. But I am still one of them. Even though I don't have the temperament they are comfortable with . . . or the attitude . . . or the personality . . . I'm one of them. I had proven myself one in Mexico. I didn't realize how much I was one of them. It surprised me to realize that. So, I convinced him. I was, in some ways, the lesser of two evils. But I was one of theirs."

Malek took all this in, in the same manner that was his way. Then he said, "That may be the reason you convinced them for you to be here . . . but it is not the reason you are here."

The guide translated.

"No. It is not the reason."

"But you know the reason, which is why you told me this story?"

"Yes."

John Lourdes knew the priest would not to ask him the reason, for that would cheat him out of coming to the moment in his own time.

Malek said to the guide, "Tell him to err on the side of caution. Tell him . . . we need him." As Hain began to speak Malek stopped him. "No . . . Just tell him to be careful. The rest might be too much of a burden. And we all have enough burdens."

"What is he saying?"

"He said . . . be careful."

"All that for two words?"

⁓

THE FIRE TEMPLE of Surakhany was a sacred place whose origins were unknown. It consisted of a walled enclosure with a square tower and portal in its eastern gate. In the center of the compound was a shrine the size of a gazebo made of plastered-over stone and brick. There were four arched portals in the shrine that faced each point of the compass, and there were four chimneys from where fire rose into the sky. In the center was a firepit where a flame continually came out of the ground.

A millennium before oil had been discovered in Baku that fire burned from naphtha leaking out of the pores of the earth. First seen by ancient caravans, word of its mystery spread. It became its own Star of Bethlehem and soon men came to that place to worship the flame itself.

Even at the last of twilight the tourists came, as did those who had made the pilgrimage to pray. Along with these was a deeply troubled Alev Temple. The dragoman had disappeared. She did not know if John and the priest were alive. She covered her eyes as if to hide from a despair she so profoundly felt.

"Alev."

Her hands came away from her face as she turned, unsure of

what she had heard. John Lourdes saw she had been crying. She went to him and grasped his vest and held it, pressing her forehead into his chest.

"You're alive," she said.

"So it seems."

"My faith was shaken. So I came here to—"

He told her the priest was fine, as was the dragoman.

"How did you find me here?"

"I followed you from the hotel."

"You followed me?"

"I need to find the German."

"He's here? In Baku?"

"Closer than that."

"I don't understand."

"Unless I have reasoned incorrectly, he will use you to try and hunt us out. That's why I'm here. To be found."

She looked, suddenly, very frightened.

"We don't have much time, you and I," he said.

"I see."

"I've left an envelope for you at the Europa. In it is information on two Turkish officers killed last night who worked with the captain. The Russian authorities should be notified."

He took her hand in his. "You seem to know this place."

"My parents came here often. When my mother was pregnant with me, she went into labor right here. My father loved to tell the story I was conceived and born here. You see, they honeymooned in Baku, of all places. Missionary doctor and nurse. There are pictures of me as a little girl . . . right here. As a matter of fact, my father named me for this place. Fire Temple . . . Alev Temple. Alev means fire. It was a silly family joke. I must admit."

"Memories." he said.

"And now . . . I have another."

Her voice seemed to fail her.

"I've been notified I'm to leave Russia," she said. "That I'm not to return anywhere within the Turkish empire. The relief agency discovered what I did in coming here. Rather than being removed, I am being reassigned to Europe. To the war in France."

He had been watching the tower gate, and there in the darkening portal, in civilian clothes, was Rittmeister Franke.

"On the dock you said something to me. I don't know if it was an Armenian phrase or—"

"I will look for you on the banks of forever."

The night had closed around them, the fires now casting their mark through the shadows. He felt the weight of the physical world upon him. He leaned down and he whispered in her ear. "We are not finished, you and I. Not by circumstance, not by fate."

She nodded, but could not speak. He held her face and kissed her.

"I am leaving now," he said.

twenty-seven

JOHN LOURDES LOGGED the outline of a pistol braced up inside the captain's coat.

"Citizen of Mexico."

"Captain."

"Lourdes . . . John Lourdes, yes? John, what would concern you more? A man who allows himself to be so easily discovered by an adversary? Or the adversary playing to that moment?"

John Lourdes reached into his vest for a cigarette which gave him time to consider the answer, "I'd weigh confidence versus strategy."

"How much of one to regard, how much of the other to disregard."

John Lourdes offered the captain the pack. He declined. John Lourdes took his time lighting the cigarette. "When we were on

211

the Tigris the pilot did not go back to notify you he'd discovered us. You either found a letter written to the missionary that he left in that room of his . . . or, you still had the compound under surveillance and you had been notified by telegraph that the girl and the dragoman were leaving for Baku. So the pilot was authorized to have at us, because your fallback position was knowing the priest's destination."

"Those would be prudent military determinations."

Alev Temple approached the gate where the men stood. She passed between them without a word. She gave John Lourdes the briefest glance, her expression revealing both fear and longing.

"Miss Temple," said Rittmeister Franke, addressing her back. "I'm sorry to hear you have been reassigned and will be leaving us for France. But I'm sure you will find ample opportunity there to express your outrage."

She passed on through the portal. With the last of her footsteps, Rittmeister Franke turned his comments to the temple.

"The land of eternal fire," he said. "I'm told it's part sham now. That the good monks sold the temple and shrine to the Baku Oil Company. And that they use jets to turn the fire on and off at will." He paused. "I know a hotel within walking distance that has quite an elegant bar. At least it did the last time I was here. It seems a better place to talk about the priest."

John Lourdes and Rittmeister Franke walked the neighborhood streets of Surakhany as if they were well-acquainted gentleman, who quietly wished the other dead.

"It seems two Turkish officers under my command disappeared. Can you shed any light on that?"

"Rumor is, their bodies weren't burned . . . like those trying to escape Van that night."

Rather disdainfully, the captain said, "There is much done here I am not in agreement with. But, like you, I am in the service of my government."

From the blocks ahead came the marshaled chorus of men's voices. They were hard and gravellish and they had cadence of a mob. It could have been a song or some kind of slogan repeated over and over. There were no instruments, and to John Lourdes' ear the voices were pitched with throaty anger and resentment.

John Lourdes and Rittmeister Franke entered a square and found themselves confronted by a sea of torches on the move. There were hundreds and hundreds of men and they looked to be supporting a river of fire on their upheld arms. Their ranks spilled up onto the sidewalks and the front steps of apartments where they called out and shouted up at the windows with a fierce urgency.

"Bolsheviks," said Rittmeister Franke.

To cross the square they had to press through the crowd, who forced on them leaflets. John Lourdes noted the men looked to be laborers and tradesmen, field workers and shopkeepers. There was an endless array of the poor and beaten down, and there were as many children as old men, and there were many of both. These were not some contingent of radicals. In Mexico they would have been defined as the *campesinos*—the people.

When they made it through this flood of bodies John Lourdes' companion looked back. "The country will fall, just as Mexico fell. You are of Mexican heritage?"

"My mother was Mexican. My father, American. As a matter of fact he had German blood in him."

THE LOBBY WAS elegant. With Persian rugs and handcarved chairs and wallpaper etched in gold. There was a bar for gentlemen, where the patrons drank quietly in candlelight from fine glasses dried and shined by white linens. There was a Victrola on a table where an attendant played recordings of classical music.

The two men sat at the teak bar. Rittmeister Franke settled on brandy. John Lourdes ordered vodka from cornel berries.

"I saw the priest in the prison courtyard," said Rittmeister Franke. "I understand why men follow him. I would myself. But now . . . it is imperative, he hand himself over."

"You have no authority in this country."

"The bomb at the Erzurum prison was set off during the midday prayer. It was a moment of vulnerability. And a good tactical move." He raised his snifter, then said, "That begs to be copied."

John Lourdes let the statement pass without comment.

"I come from a long line of Junkers," said Rittmeister Franke. "That is what they call aristocratic landowners in eastern Prussia. Even if those landowners are long since impoverished. My family is from the same region as Bismarck. The 'blood and iron' period of unification. In our family it was demanded the eldest son join the army. I was not the eldest."

John Lourdes tapped his cigarette on the bar to tighten up the tobacco. He lit it. He stared at the dark cabinetry where the liquor was shelved. "I was a railroad detective, and a member of the Bureau of Investigation. Domestic crime, border security. My mother crossed a desert on foot to reach the United States. My father was a criminal and a common assassin." He then looked at the captain, "But biographies don't count for much in a bloodletting, do they?"

Rittmeister Franke studied his opponent openly.

"He has at best a hundred men . . . possibly two hundred, who will follow him on his nation building journey. He is a cleric, and nothing more. North of here, in the mountains, there are over a thousand men. I brought Kurds from the prisons . . . and Turkish officers from the Special Organization . . . There are men from the Ukraine . . . and there are Tartars from Baku. Seven hundred, at least. These are all peoples who disdain each other. But they have one thing in common, hatred for the Armenian. He is like the Jew in that way. The Armenian-Tartar war was fought in Baku. I was here then in 1906, on a military scouting mission. There are photographs of the dead, of ruined oilfields, mosques burned, churches destroyed. The men in the hills lost fathers in that war, lost brothers, lost sons in that war. They have been sharpening their hearts for a moment like this. They know Russia will fall to the Bolsheviks. And that there will be chaos. It is clear the Armenian wants a homeland. But if one is to be created, the people living there now will not want to live under them. The priest is trying to defy *realpolitik*. Reports say the Americans wanted him to help support the British in their fight south of Baghdad. That would have been more pragmatic. Citizen of Mexico, understand . . . this region is nothing but hatreds. And those are the only eternal fires."

The two men stared at each other through a mirror behind the bar.

"The munitions you needed didn't arrive," said Rittmeister Franke. "Did your superiors tell you they were intercepted? Intelligence suggests your government came to a political rationale not to support Malek in Russia. That the time may come when they need to have good relations with a *Bolshevik* regime. It's possible that bringing Malek here was just a military diversion, a front to maintain influence with the Armenian people. Malek may have more value as a martyr." The captain then turned sympathetic. "I can't believe you fought as hard as you did to cross Persia while knowing that. Which indicates, your superiors lied to you."

John Lourdes said nothing. He understood. The captain's immediate purpose was to induce doubt—if you want to defeat the man, you must first poison the mind. John Lourdes thought back to a night in Mexico, near the end, when he and his father sat in a hotel bar, not unlike the bar he sat in now, and he told his father, "What is required . . . but to do justice."

John Lourdes turned to the captain. There was a quiet fierceness about him. "The priest and I are going to take the fight to you. And hard. And it's not because of orders . . . or the will of a government." He paused, then said, "But because women and children were left to suffer and die in a desert. Because horseshoes were hammered into a man's feet. And because somewhere men sat together and willfully decided to rewrite the Ten Commandments."

Rittmeister Frank politely finished his brandy. He stood. He took money from his pocket. "Do you know the Armenikend?"

"I do not."

"It is the Armenian quarter just outside of the Icheri Sheher. There is a bazaar there not unlike the one alongside the prison at Erzurum. If the priest does not give himself over tomorrow morning to me here, midday at the bazaar he will be taught a lesson."

For a brief moment he sat again. "You have been excellent at escaping and eluding . . . but eventually that must end."

⁓

AT THE IRONWORKS John Lourdes sat with Malek and Mr. Ordina at a table with maps of Baku and the surrounding countryside spread out on the rough hewn planks. Mr. Ordina marked areas in the hills where he felt a large number of Tartars could be encamped.

More critical, however, was the imminent threat at the Armenikend. Was it fact, or a means to lure Malek there for capture or assassination. The German knew the priest would not give himself over.

Mr. Ordina made an appeal they approach Russian authorities and have Rittmeister Franke arrested as a spy and saboteur. John Lourdes was against it, as undoubtedly the captain's replacement was already there on the ground.

For Malek, the German seemed a smart and determined man and courageous enough to take acute risks. Still, better the devil you know, than the one you don't. Another fact was becoming evidently clear: a confrontation was not only inevitable, it was imperative.

When they heard the watchman call out and the gate swing open, they knew it to be the guide returning with what they hoped was good news. He had been in the darkness at the Fire Temple, guarding John Lourdes, and then it had been left to him to follow the German.

He was exhausted and covered with a strange ashen dirt. He asked for liquor and one of the maps. He said he was lucky to have gotten back alive and he used his lit *chibouk* as a pointer. The German and two other Europeans had left the hotel and ridden out the peninsula. Their route had taken them past the oilfields and through a black and barren country Hain knew to be the land of the mud volcanoes. That was the cakey textured earth that clung to his flesh and clothes. The last glimpse he had of the three they were following a dry course up into the hills. There, for a brief moment, they flashed across the face of the moon.

In the halflife of that kerosene lamp, the somber and determined faces of the men around the map, John Lourdes could only hope to himself this was a first step in scaling the mortal disadvantage that confronted them.

In the outlying districts of Baku, many Armenian homes had been abandoned and left to grim decay. They had moved to a lower section of the Armenikend that was built on marshy and fever-plagued land near Black Town. Armenian shopkeepers and merchants had also shut down their businesses in the Icheri Sheher and moved to the Armenikend, for the hatred and violence the Tartar exacted against them was unrelenting. And the fact the Armenian was more well off only added to their fury. In a country where Armenians served faithfully in the army, they were despised.

The bazaar was set up on a plaza where half a dozen narrow streets made entry. John Lourdes found a flat rooftop where he and the guide could survey the scene below. Hain was told to watch for the German or those with him the night before. When the guide asked John Lourdes what he thought the German had in mind, was it a trap, John Lourdes did not answer. His was a pre-monition he did not want to give voice to.

As noon came upon them, the square was heavily trafficked. People of the quarter pressed past mule-drawn carts and camels strapped down with trade. The sun was cruelly hot upon the roof and no less so on the tents that covered the trading stalls.

It was the guide who first saw something that aroused his suspicion, "Efendi!" He sat and pointed, "There, by the church. A wagon . . . tarped. One grey horse. The man in the box seat I recognize."

Field glasses swept the pavilion and the church. John Lourdes focused in on the wagon. A European sat on the box seat where men and women with trade made their slow way past. John Lourdes could make out a shadow inside the wagon on the tarp hooding. In the bed of that wagon he saw just the tops of wood and scrap piles where the shadow sat huddled over. The European on the box seat looked to his watch then intensely to the square. When he stepped down from the wagon and started away quickly

John Lourdes knew his premonition was about to be proved true.

John Lourdes leapt to his feet, he ordered the guide, "The men in the wagon. They are to be followed to whatever end."

He jumped from the roof to the one below and from there to the ground where he stumbled to his knees.

"Efendi?" the guide yelled from the ledge above.

"To whatever end," John Lourdes shouted, before he was gone running towards the square.

John Lourdes never heard the detonation, nor the wails of those taken apart by chain mail and blades of wood. When he came to, there was the taste of blood and iron in his mouth. He felt for the ground. He had no idea when and how he came to be on his hands and knees. He had all he could do to keep from keeling over. He managed to raise his head and there before him a scene of mass butchery. Men and beast alike, crying out or dead, the bodies smoldering and scattered across the square.

twenty-eight

E HAD GOTTEN to his feet, but was uncertain how. The terrible mayhem around him seemed miles away. He pieced together that he had been knocked unconscious by part of a wagon hull that cut a path through the crowd like a plough shovel. Upon returning to the ironworks he was still dazed. The gateman ran to the office to notify Mr. Ordina as foundrymen stared at this slumped and tottering figure riding past in blood-stained clothes.

John Lourdes was alone in the barracks sitting at the table when Malek entered with Mr. Ordina and the dragoman. The blood told part of the story, John Lourdes' notebook would tell the rest. He wanted Mr. Ordina to write down what he dictated, and what he dictated was the bombing in the square.

The dragoman poured John Lourdes a drink, but his hands were too unsteady so it was left to the old one to hold the glass to his lips. He spoke haltingly at first, then an urgency took over until John Lourdes was finally possessed by outrage. When finished dictating he asked the dragoman to ride to the Europa Hotel and see to it those pages were delivered to either Alev Temple or the newspaperman who had come with them to Baku.

The priest and John Lourdes sat by each other silently until long after the others had gone. At twilight John Lourdes leaned over and fingered the bandoleer the priest wore, until he came to the crucifix with its one broken cross beam.

"I had one like this," said John Lourdes, his voice a mere whisper. "My mother gave it to me. My father shot off part of a beam in a moment of contempt. She would say there was only two paths in life a person can take . . . That of the good thief, or that of the bad thief." His voice fell away. "My father . . ."

John Lourdes took a long and emptying breath, he stood and undid his shoulder holster. He removed his vest and washed the blood of others from his arms and throat and face. He changed shirts then went and stood in the open doorway as evening descended. He spoke not another word until the guide returned.

Hain called out from the saddle, "Efendi . . . was that a bomb I heard while running from the square?"

"It was. Do you have news? Do you know where they have gone?"

"I have been close enough to relieve myself on their slippers."

Hain leaned out from the saddle. He put a hand on John Lourdes' shoulder and looked him over. "I worried for you today, efendi."

⁀

THE GUIDE LED John Lourdes and the priest out the peninsula and through the land of mud volcanoes.

At the Yanardagh—Fire Mountain—methane seeped from the earth, and a flame sawed violently out of the hillside a hundred meters high. They passed beneath its fury shadowing the trucks of wagons that scored the gravelly reef of the slopeface. Up along black and serrated ridgetops the guide pointed out campfires strung through a succession of valleys.

They had found the enemy. They studied the circles of fire and dark clusters of horses picketed along the streams till the coming light rendered it unsafe.

By dawn they had descended out of the hills and were passing through a landscape where the ground was cracked and dry like the skin of lizard. A slender road made its way through glacial pools of mud and past volcanic pyramids oozing a gruelish liquid that bubbled with toxic gases. The earth in that place bore craterish cysts that stank of methane and naphtha.

They came to the beginnings of an oil field that ran to the sea on a slender isthmus. The road was deserted and the priest asked them to dismount. They stood together in a Caspian dawn.

"We have seen," he said. "And now?"

The guide asked this of John Lourdes.

"There's a thousand men up there. Eight hundred anyway. Wouldn't you say?"

"At least eight hundred, efendi."

"And Malek has what . . . a hundred and fifty citizens. Men of good will."

"We have the night, efendi. And we know where they are."

"Yes." John Lourdes looked to the priest, who waited. "Tell him we'll make a plan. Go in when it's dark. Punish them as best we can. Run off their mounts. Bomb them, burn them. And get out."

Hain told this to the priest who asked, "And then?"

"And then, efendi?"

"Then? Retreat back into the hills till we get supplied with money and munitions."

When he heard this Malek shook his head saying no.

"I know what he wants," said John Lourdes. "He wants a goddamn dog fight. And he wants a pit dug, less won't do. They do have dog fights in this country, don't they?"

"They have dog fights, efendi."

The guide relayed this conversation to the priest.

Malek slipped his hands under the bandoleer and clasped them together against his chest. "I understand through my actions I have failed as a priest. That I have fallen from the true morality of peace. I am resigned to that fact. I know the more I succeed through warfare, the more my eternal soul is at risk. I am resigned to that, also." He undid his hands and took hold of the bandoleer. He then touched the holster. "I have chosen . . . *chosen* . . . to be the agent of these souls, for one purpose."

Malek squatted and picked up a handful of road dust. "They say only God can create man, but that is half so. Man creates a nation, which is man. And a nation is created only in part by ideas, is created only in part by laws." He stood and let the dust slip from his palm. "It is also created through the language of moments. Threats defied, persecutions endured, spirits that will neither rest nor succumb, by actions that determine the course of souls.

"There are moments such as these written in all histories. I have read of them from the time of Rome and Greece. From Arabia and Russia. These moments proclaim who the people of those places truly are. And it does not matter if they are celebrated or barely greeted in their time with a word, but that they are true. And I am sure there are such moments as these in America . . . In your Tig-ziz. I am sure there were such moments told to you as a boy. That you carry now."

John Lourdes quietly nodded. "We have such moments. I have such moments," he said.

"Make the fight."

John Lourdes took off his hat, he swept that arm outward. "Look around you. It's open country. They'll run us down."

The priest grabbed the bandoleer and shook it. He was demanding a fight. John Lourdes walked to his mount and retrieved his field glasses. He began to study the country. It was as he suspected, defenseless. He kept panning the glasses, searching for a tactical advantage.

From where they stood a road led down into the isthmus. He noted there were about a dozen working oil derricks, but many more lay in ruin next to their derelict housing structures. There were others yet that were partly toppled. He asked the guide if the priest could tell them of this. The priest answered how this isthmus had been the site of fighting during the war between the Armenian and the Tartar.

It was the rising of the light and the wind blowing through the high weeds that caused John Lourdes to catch sight of piping by a rusted derrick about a hundred yards out.

He swung into the saddle and headed off without so much as a word. The derrick was on a slight rise that ascended gradually along the road he came from. To reach the derrick he had to cross a wooden span of about ten meters. It had been built over a trench, and in the trench was a pipeline. What he had seen in the weeds was an inlet station and flow tank that connected directly to the pipeline in the trench. A trench, he now noted, furrowed across the width of the isthmus.

He dismounted. From where he stood the isthmus sloped gently down to the sea. What lay between was a half mile of irrefutable testimony to human folly and waste. Ghostly derricks, huge pools of black oil, abandoned barracks, crumbling sheds, hulls of rotted wagons that looked like planters for wild brush. The road went past a street of forgotten buildings falling down upon themselves, and huge storage tanks, one with a side torn away so you could see the Caspian right through it. The derricks that were pumping were connected by a lattice of trenches piping the crude up to the flow station where John Lourdes stood.

Beyond that, at the tip of the isthmus was a graveyard of vessels. Barges, a tug, what looked to be a schooner, all lay sunk in the shallows like grey corpses. On the beach was a huge tanker that must have run aground during a storm, its rusting bow rose up out of the water and shouldered high above the sandy embankment.

The guide and the priest rode up to John Lourdes.

"Efendi, what is all this?"

John Lourdes saw there was only a skeleton crew working the derricks far down the isthmus. It would be easy enough to run that few out.

"Efendi?"

"I want you to see that derrick . . . the trench . . . that's an oil pipeline. See how it crosses the isthmus to those storage drums. In the trench oil has leaked out over years, see those pools."

"I see it all, efendi."

"We start the fight in the hills. We try to lure them here. We retreat back down toward the beach. They follow. Then we detonate this derrick and those drums and the trench. We could create a firestorm across the isthmus worthy of God. They'll be trapped."

The guide looked and thought and spoke, "And we also."

"That . . . is what will make the trap work."

Malek dismounted. He demanded to know what was being said.

"Tell him," said John Lourdes. "Tell him we can make the fight here . . . but most, if not all, will die. And I believe we will still be defeated."

The guide told this to the priest, who in turn looked down at the bandoleer and hunted through the beads and rosaries until he found the crucifix with the simple broken cross beam. This he undid, then walked to John Lourdes and strung the leather that held the cross through a button hole in John Lourdes' vest. He asked the guide something, and the guide replied, "Defeated."

Malek held the cross and said to John Lourdes, "Defeated."

Then the priest spoke to the guide, who said to John Lourdes, "That was handed to you by a dying boy at the camp, was it not?"

"Yes," said John Lourdes.

"And today, after the bombing, at the ironworks, you searched it out."

"Yes," said John Lourdes.

"The priest says he understands you well. That you and he are both of the same wilderness. And he wants to know . . . now. Are you prepared to make the fight here?"

John Lourdes looked out upon the isthmus. From the first brutal murders on the quay in Constantinople, to the bombing at the Armenikend, he had been witness to the future, and the stark barbarity that gave birth to it. He saw that a new level of infamy *had* been ushered into all their lives. And he understood, they did not have the makings for a long fight, so a single and terrifying act would have to be enough to exact their will.

"We'll make the fight here," said John Lourdes.

twenty-nine

A LITTLE OVER ONE hundred men gathered up around the priest in a camp north of the Baladzhary Station. Malek spoke with passion about the rich history of their people and the daunting task they were about to embark upon to fulfill that history. The men then armed themselves and rode off with the guide leading them.

John Lourdes took the dragoman and twenty of the volunteers to the isthmus. He'd mapped out where charges were to be set, when and how they were to be detonated. He showed the dragoman how a defensive plan was to be executed, where fires were to be started, and when the derrick crews should be driven from the isthmus. They ended at the beach, where the tanker lay upon the shore. It was there, if any of their number survived, that the last of the strategy would be played out.

John Lourdes joined the priest in the mountains. From there

they could look down upon a starfield of Tartar campfires. They waited as the volunteers muffled their horses' heads, then secretly marched along the crest trails to their positions. Alone in that uneasy darkness, John Lourdes quietly addressed the priest:

"There is something I want to speak of. I don't know if it's good or not, the fact you can't understand me. The other night on the foundry roof, I answered to myself why I'm here. One word says it . . . Forgiveness. I have been to a place like this once in Mexico, with my father. A man I meant to see dead . . . who I wanted to see dead. A man I led to his death.

"Sometimes there is little reward to what is just. I was dying there, in Mexico, and my father tricked me into staying alive, by giving up life himself. He set a trap for me with his own existence as bait, like a trap we are setting tonight. Yes, like tonight. He proved to be a man I could not ultimately outsmart or outthink. A man like yourself. I'm am here to justify his act, and in the doing ask he forgive me . . . for wanting him dead, for taking him to his end. I understand . . . Please, forgive me."

Those were things he had never said. Not even to himself, for it was the acknowledgement of some ultimate debt. His voice could not even scale the emotions, so the words just broke. But the priest heard. He didn't need to know words. He had been ordained with a calling to put everything that was said, aside, and just see.

The priest put out a hand, resting it on John Lourdes' shoulder. In the possession of just a few dark moments they sat like that, then the priest whispered, "Brother, sometimes the suffering, is suffering enough. I hope this for us all. The wilderness . . . We will cross it together."

There came the slightest tricklings of gravel where the guide stepped from the shadows. He spoke in a whisper. "All is ready, efendi."

John Lourdes reached for the flare gun which lay on a rock beside him. He wondered, had the guide heard him? He stood and walked to the edge of the cliff face. All was still down that long succession of valleys. Just the glow of smoldering campfires topped by thin runners of smoke.

He looked to the priest, who nodded. John Lourdes aimed and fired. A flare lanced across the sky, and in the next moments came the ferocious report of gunfire.

Down through that gallery of ledges John Lourdes could see the flashpoint of the Enfield gunbarrels. The explosions started soon after. About a dozen volunteers with grenade rifles were firing down into the camps. Horses had begun to stampede, the gray storm of their dust rising into the night.

John Lourdes watched through field glasses for the first signs of organized resistance. Shadows were scattering from the quake of dynamite. A fire was blowing down through the length of one valley and he caught the spectre of horsemen against the flames massing together and then at a full gallop starting up a trail through the cliff face.

"They're on the move!" shouted John Lourdes.

The guide gathered up their mounts. John Lourdes walked to the ledge. He fired off another flare, quickly following with a second. The priest was already mounted when John Lourdes swung up into the saddle. The volunteers had seen the signal, and the firing along the ledges had ceased. They had gathered up and were coming on hard in small mounted packs and passing John Lourdes on the trail out of the mountains. The retreat had begun.

Already there were wounded, stooped over or clinging to their saddles. When the last of that citizen company had vanished, the three started down the rocky slopeface at an even trot. About a quarter mile further on they pulled up at a place along the precipice where the rocky trail was wide enough to be taken at a full gallop.

John Lourdes and the guide dismounted by a stake in the ground marking where dynamite had been braced against the stone facing. The priest remained mounted and kept watch. John Lourdes hooked up the charge and the guide reeled the cable down that shaly roadway about fifty meters.

The priest called out. Along the escarpment a heavily armed band of Tartars was pressing after them. They appeared as a single entity with tunics flowing wildly under the moonlight. As they trampled down that stake John Lourdes detonated the charge. The passage and part of the shelf face blew out over the canyon, taking mounted riders with it. They fell into the silent void turning like great stone weights, their screams trailing off desperately till they were no more.

John Lourdes and the guide remounted. They and the priest made their way down through straits of wooded trail until John Lourdes reined in the Arabian and came about. With field glasses he could make out bleak shapes against the gray stone. It was a detachment, maybe a hundred or so Tartars, on the hunt, proceeding with caution.

The mountains fell away to darkness. Their descent all rumor and shadow. At opportune places along the way John Lourdes would have them halt and send out a volley of gunfire, or leave a lit stick of dynamite to blow away a piece of road, slowing the pursuit to a fateful walk.

As planned the volunteers waited in a long swale at the footing of the mountains. The edges of the horizon to the east had begun to lighten when Malek rode among them with John Lourdes and the guide. The wounded were being tended, their number had been struck down by a near dozen. John Lourdes could see in the faces of the men they understood the fight to come would be swift and merciless.

The guide knew first the enemy was upon them. He did not need field glasses—the subtle motion along the haw and withers of the mounts was enough.

"Efendi, they are here."

John Lourdes took to his field glasses. From the Caspian horsemen in blue tunics were coming, like a wave of ocean upon the earth. "Have everyone mount and be ready," he said.

The guide told the priest, and the priest commanded the men. John Lourdes' horse was beside the guide's. Before he swung up into the saddle he asked Hain, "In Van . . . you chose to come. You said—"

"I know what you are asking. Why am I here? Efendi . . . every man is entitled to his secrets. And his fires."

He now understood the guide had overheard him talking to the priest the night before. John Lourdes then rode up out of the swale, and the men followed. He kept looking to the west.

"Efendi . . . from the mountains."

The detachment that had been at their rear was fanning out over a ridge, the pumice rising from the force of their hooves. The riders fired their rifles into the air to let the Armenian volunteers know the raw of combat was approaching.

John Lourdes did not want to retreat too soon to the isthmus. He wanted it to look as if the priest and his men were driven there, so he kept his field glasses to the west, for that was the last and only avenue of escape.

The men herded up around him and the wind coming from the sea blew violently that morning and the grass bent then crested against the saddles. Hats were lost, and the coats of the volunteers spread up and out like blackened wings. What the wind would do with the fires to come, thought John Lourdes.

He watched the sun inch across the landscape. He stayed with its slow and irrevocable journey whispering, "Come on . . ." until the light finally flooded over the plain and he could see Rittmeister Frank and the main body of men.

"You have been excellent at eluding and escaping," he had told John Lourdes at the bar, "but eventually that must end."

thirty

*T*HAT SMALL COMPANY of men pressed on through the high grass running from the enemy toward that unearthly place of volcanic mud and cracked strata, taking a slender road through its parched landscape toward the oil derrick on the rise at the point of the isthmus.

The first Tartars to close upon them were those coming out of the hills. They were not so formidable a number, and John Lourdes had the men halt and cover the road.

They spread across that cremated area, kneeling, lying prone, their rifles shouldered. John Lourdes had chosen this place to make a momentary stand. He'd had the dragoman plant dynamite there and when the Tartars swept past that spot, the charge was detonated.

Humans as well as beasts were catapulted. Craters of naphtha burst into flame, the ground began to smoke. The remaining Tartars tried to outflank the riflemen but their mounts could not traverse the rivers of mud. They slipped and struggled and the viscous liquid clung to their legs that buckled or seized up, and the horsemen were naked targets collapsing under a barrage of gunfire to die where they would blacken and fossilize.

From the east and the west the enemy came on with punishing resolve. Those with the swiftest mounts were already making their cumbersome way through that place where the ground was like cracked pottery. John Lourdes ordered the guide to have the men pull back beyond the derricks. Their dust swept up and through that steel and wood well tower, hooves clopping across the timbered span above the trench as they retreated into the isthmus. The three remained by the derrick to watch the oncoming assault when a flare cut across the sky.

With field glasses John Lourdes found Rittmeister Franke. The captain was studying the distance with uncanny vigilance. For a moment the two men watched each other across the battlefield. The captain was slowing the attack, while scanning the landscape for threats.

"He's reading us," said John Lourdes. "He senses something isn't right."

The priest called out to the guide asking what was wrong and Hain swept his rifle across the frontier where the attack had stilled. The priest rose from his saddle. He saw, and understood. He eased back down and spoke with decided calm. "Tell our friend here, I will bring them. Leave me. Both of you. Do as I say, and hurry! I will be enough."

This John Lourdes did not want to do, leave the priest, but the priest ordered him. He and the guide then galloped down the slope to where the volunteers waited.

Malek turned his mount toward the derrick standing at the pitch of the rise. John Lourdes watched as he removed something from his robe. With the wave of a hand, a flag shook loose. Homespun and ragged, with the sunlight pouring through the struts and shorings of that well tower, Malek held the flag aloft.

The firing had been at long range but John Lourdes now saw the several hundred riders by the Caspian surge toward the isthmus. Whether Rittmeister Franke had signaled the order, or it was a spontaneous reaction to the priest's defiant act John Lourdes would never know.

The Armenians spread out among the ruins and dismounted. The priest rejoined John Lourdes and the guide. They remained mounted to maintain order and command as long as possible, or until they were dead.

The first wave of horseman broke over the rise, the next poured across that tiny bridge, or leapt the pipeline trench. Rittmeister Franke took up a position from where he could survey the isthmus. They had committed themselves to finality.

From the western edge of the isthmus there was an explosion. A concussion went through the bones of the earth and the ground beneath the riders shook. Whorls of smoke and consumed oil rose above the peninsula in a hellish cloud. Storage tanks had been detonated by the dragoman and a handful of volunteers. Before the pursuers could recognize fully what had happened the derrick on the rise blew. And when it did, it took part of the crest with it.

A battery of riders was immolated. Others were strewn about the rise burnt or dying. Their horses ablaze rushed wild and headlong across that ghost town of ruin and debris trying to escape their death. Flames from the derrick rose to such heights bits of detritus and oil fell in a scalding rain across the isthmus. Pieces of iron sheeting that had been transported to that place by wagon were thrown to the sea.

The crude that had leaked into the pipeline trench was ignited by the bridge. The pipe itself blew out, triggering a tunnel of fire down the length of that ditch and across the isthmus to the burning tanks. The pipe kept blowing where seams had been welded shut. Flames welled up out of that trench torching the brush and summer grass. The Tartar horsemen saw they were trapped and some thought they could escape by whipping their mounts to leap the fire. Others sought out the last openings in the blaze the wind had yet to close. But the wind was carrying the day, and the ground on both sides of that hollowed causeway began to burn out of control, spreading across the isthmus and down to the sea.

Everywhere there were men dying, and there were men dead. A small pocket of Armenian volunteers fighting to escape the burning grass were trampled under a wave of tunicked riders. They came out of the smoke like a feverish nightmare streaked with oil and ash and all before them went under their hooves. They fired down into the faces of the fallen and they rode on through reefs of smoke to disappear.

John Lourdes could see the battle was nearing its end. Only a handful of stragglers were left, maybe two dozen, trying to make their way to the beach. He scanned the huge storage tanks by a vast pool of oil in the middle of the isthmus. The dragoman was to have set a charge there. It should have detonated by now. John Lourdes could not pinpoint the spot well enough through the smoke. He signaled the guide, he intended to ride back and detonate it himself, when he saw the captain.

Rittmeister Franke was still mounted, still in command. He had a bandana around a head wound, his shirt was bloody. He was giving orders to his chiefs and as he scanned the ground before him another derrick blew near the rocky shoreline. Its housing had been consumed by fire, and when the well detonated part of the structure came loose from its moorings and was slung across acres of scrap iron like a ferris wheel of flames.

Through the smoke, John Lourdes started back up the isthmus toward the storage tanks. He was galloping through a vast pool of oil when the Arabian was shot from under him. He was there one moment then lost to a world of fire the next. The guide saw, and he pointed with his rifle shouting to the priest. They kicked their mounts forward and plunged into those choking latitudes to try and reach him.

John Lourdes lay at the edge of the sinkhole using the dead Arabian as a barricade. Tartars were trying to ride down on him when the guide and the priest galloped up through that swamping oil. The priest and the guide dismounted. Seared particles rained down on the black surface of that pond where the three men gathered up. Streaked with crude and ash, they fought their way up from the pond, the air a black haze that horsemen charged through. In the chaos, one of the three fell mortally wounded.

John Lourdes and the priest carried the guide into the shadow of the storage tank where the charge was to have been set. He had been shot through the sternum and one of his lungs was already drowning.

They sat him upright against the tank wall. He stared at the wound then at the faces of the last men he would ever see on earth.

"Efendi," he said, "I am thirty-three years old. I fear I will be thirty-three forever."

John Lourdes took hold of the guide's arm. He went to speak, but Malek shook him and pointed. Not ten feet away lay the body of dragoman by the unfinished charge.

"Prepare it," ordered the priest. He shoved John Lourdes. "Prepare it!"

John Lourdes understood, without the knowing, and crawled to the body of the dragoman for the detonator.

Malek took the guide's hands in his own. "When you are at Abraham's tent . . . and are one of the honored offering a drink of water to those who will come after . . . If I am proven worthy of that place, it is you I will look for, you alone. And I will kneel before you, and it will be my hope you offer me to drink . . ."

When John Lourdes crawled back with the detonator, the priest was whispering into Hain's ear, and the guide was nodding as best he could. John Lourdes pulled himself next to Hain, his back propped against the tank. He had the detonator in his lap, all wired and ready. He waved the priest away, "Go on. I can take care of this. Go on!"

The guide was looking at the priest when he reached out and put a hand on the detonator.

"Efendi . . . Let me finish my journey. Go with the priest."

Malek had already risen and gotten hold of a Tartar horse. It was wounded but looked still able to run. The guide was having difficulty pulling the detonator toward him, so John Lourdes lifted it and set it in his lap. He sat a moment, then went to stand. Hesitating, he pointed at the amulet Hain wore with its painted eye.

"I will it to you, efendi," said the guide.

John Lourdes removed the talisman from the guide's blouse and ran to the priest.

The Tartars were sweeping the isthmus. There was no longer resistance. Everywhere were the dead, everywhere the wounded. About a dozen volunteers had made the shore and were huddled up in the sand behind the grounded tanker.

When the guide pressed down the plunger, the side of the storage tank blew out, and so too the tanks in the field around it were blown.

A tidal wave of fire went down through the heart of that isthmus. Everything in its path was incinerated. The street of abandoned sheds and barracks, there one moment, gone the next. The dead and wounded, flesh one moment, ash the next. Slicks of oil, evaporated in a breath. Sheets of metal lying in the brush, burned so hot the earth beneath melted. That wall of fire hit the tanker with such force the steel monolith literally moved. It rocked ever so slightly, the hull groaning, as the fire rose and rose and rose until the sky was gone.

epilogue

HE WORK OF Alev Temple and Carson Ammons, the newspaperman who had been with her at the Baskahle Road and Baku, was published as a book of eyewitness accounts and photographs on the atrocities committed in the name of the Turkish government against the Armenian population.

That volume, along with others, such as the memoir *Ravished Armenia*, which was made into a motion picture starring Anna Q. Nilsson, became part of the international literature on that infamous chapter of history. Many of these works were deemed "gross exaggerations" or "sensational lies." Carson Ammons, when interviewed, answered those claims by stating—Let the reader discover the truth for themselves.

AT THE END of the Great War, with the help of President Woodrow Wilson, an Armenian republic was created. The young nation was under constant military threat from its bordering neighbors. With the invasion of the 11th Red Army, the government was crushed, and Armenia forced into the Soviet Union.

In 1991, as the USSR broke apart, Armenia was the first non-Baltic nation to declare its independence.

⁓

ALSO IN 1920, the 11th Army marched upon Baku. All property there was seized, all prior ownership voided. The oil fields became the sovereign domain of the USSR.

As it had been secretly planned by the Triple Entente, the *vilayets* of Basra and Baghdad, then finally Mosul, were cobbled into a new nation that would serve as a buffer zone and puppet state for the British, which would allow them to maintain control of the Basra oilfields and protect the gateway to India and the East.

That nation, of course, was called Iraq.

⁓

IN A STATEMENT from Adolf Hitler on August 22, 1939, in response to concerns about his plan to destroy every man, woman and child of Polish derivation, the Chancellor of Nazi Germany wrote, "Who, after all, speaks today of the annihilation of the Armenians?"

In 1942, Raphael Lempkin, a Warsaw barrister, coined the term "genocide," in part, because of the atrocities committed by the Turkish government against the Armenian population.

As FOR THE violent engagement fought upon that small isthmus along the eastern shore of the Absheron Peninsula in 1915, John Lourdes had, in fact, conceived a plan for escape, if all were lost.

A handful of small skiffs powered by oars had been secretly cached beyond the grounded tanker. A dozen men had survived the inferno. They took to the water, then finally the boats, under the cover of fire and smoke. Among the twelve were the priest known as Malek, and a young man from the state of Texas, whose reports detailing this incident, and discovered in 1937 among the lost files of the Creel Committee, constituted the basis of this book.

acknowledgments

To Deirdre Stephanie and the late, great Brutarian . . . to G.G. and
L.S. . . . . Jim Kelley . . . Kelley and Hall . . . Pauline Neuwirth and
Beth Metrick . . . Catherine Casalino . . . Special thanks to Tracy
Falco at Universal for the filmic opportunity . . . And finally to my
steadfast friend and ally, and a master at navigating the madness,
Donald V. Allen.